Also by Da

POETRY

Hush (1976)
The Shore (1980)
No Heaven (1985)
Terraces of Rain: An Italian Sketchbook (1991)
Study for the World's Body (1994)
In the Pines: Lost Poems, 1972–1997 (1998; 2016)
The Red Leaves of Night (1999)
Prism (2002)
The Face: A Novella in Verse (2004)
The Auroras (2012)

LIMITED EDITIONS

For Lerida (1973)
The Olive Grove (1980)
A Folio of Lost Worlds (1981)
The Man in the Yellow Gloves (1985)
The Orange Piano (1987)
A New Shade of Blue (1998)
Peruvian Portals (2013)
The Window: Poems, 1998–2012 (2014)

PROSE

Where the Angels Come Toward Us:
Selected Essays, Reviews, and Interviews (1995)

EDITOR

The Selected Levis, by Larry Levis (2000)
American Hybrid: A Norton Anthology of New Poetry
(with Cole Swensen; 2009)
The Darkening Trapeze: Last Poems of Larry Levis (2016)

THE
LAST TROUBADOUR

THE
LAST
TROUBADOUR

New and Selected Poems

David St. John

An Imprint of HarperCollins*Publishers*

HarperCollins books may be purchased for educational, business, or sales promotional use. For information, please e-mail the Special Markets Department at SPsales@harpercollins.com.

A hardcover edition of this book was published in 2017 by Ecco, an imprint of HarperCollins Publishers.

FIRST ECCO PAPERBACK EDITION PUBLISHED 2018.

Designed by Suet Yee Chong

Library of Congress Cataloging-in-Publication Data has been applied for.

ISBN 978-0-06-264094-9

18 19 20 21 22   LSC   10 9 8 7 6 5 4 3 2 1

In memory of Howard Moss

Contents

I.

Selected Poems
(1976–2012)

Slow Dance   *3*

Iris   *7*

Dolls   *9*

Gin   *11*

Hush   *13*

The Shore   *14*

Blue Waves   *17*

The Avenues   *19*

Guitar   *21*

Elegy   *22*

The Boathouse   *24*

Hotel Sierra   *26*

Song Without Forgiveness   *30*

Until the Sea Is Dead   *31*

A Hard & Noble Patience   *37*

The Day of the Sentry   *38*

Desire   *40*

The Reef   *41*

Woman & Leopard   *42*

Shadow   *46*

Meridian   *47*

The Swan at Sheffield Park   *49*

The Man in the Yellow Gloves   *55*

Leap of Faith   *63*

Terraces of Rain   *64*

Last Night with Rafaella   *66*

I Know   *69*

Lucifer in Starlight   *70*

Merlin   *73*

The Figure *You*   *75*

Night   *76*

Rhapsody   *77*

Chevalier d'Or   *78*

Stories   *79*

Red Wheat: Montana   *80*

Beeches   *81*

The Park   *82*

The Red Leaves of Night   *83*

The Aurora of the New Mind   *84*

Gypsy Davy's Flute of Rain   *86*

The Aurora of the Lost Dulcimer   *88*

Late Oracle Sonnet   *89*

In the High Country   *90*

From a Bridge   *91*

Without Mercy, the Rains Continued   *92*

Hungry Ghost   *93*

Creque Alley   *96*

Reckless Wing   *98*

The Empty Frame   *99*

The Auroras   *104*

II.

The Way It Is

(New Poems)

Where He Came Down   *119*

Hot Night in Akron   *120*

The Way It Is *122*

When My Baby Rocks the Funk *123*

The One Who Should Write My Elegy Is Dead *124*

Vineyard *125*

Lucky *127*

Generation *130*

The Last Troubadour *132*

Alexandr Blok *133*

To a Story *134*

My Life as Sandoz Mescaline *136*

Evangeline & Her Sisters *137*

An Ecclesiastical Sketchbook *138*

Above Sunset *140*

Backstreets *141*

Equivalents *142*

Aperture *144*

Emanations *146*

The Darkroom *154*

The Stones of Venice *155*

Silver & Black *156*

Pasternak & the Snowy Heron *158*

In Bangkok *159*

Little Sur *160*

To Those Who Have Asked Anna *161*

Damian's Tale *162*

The Old Wave *164*

The Black Jaguar *165*

Script for the Lost Reflection *166*

Acknowledgments

Some of the poems in this collection first appeared in:

The Academy of American Poets "Poem-a-Day": Alexandr Blok.

The American Poetry Review: A Hard & Noble Patience; Aperture; Reckless Wing; Hot Night in Akron; Silver & Black; To Those Who Have Asked Anna.

American Poets: *The Journal of the Academy of American Poets*: Above Sunset.

Antaeus: Slow Dance; Song Without Forgiveness; The Day of the Sentry; The Man in the Yellow Gloves; Terraces of Rain; I Know; Merlin; The Figure *You*; Night.

Blackbird: The Darkroom.

Crazy Horse: Meridian.

The Denver Quarterly: Lucifer in Starlight; Stories; The Auroras ("Ghost Aurora"; "Aurore Parisienne"; "Père Lachaise"; "The Book"; "Dark Aurora")

FIELD: The Auroras ("Dawn Aurora"; "Lago di Como"; "Autumn"; "Florentine Aurora"); Pasternak & the Snowy Heron; The Old Wave.

The Gettysburg Review: Last Night with Rafaella.

Great River Review: My Life as Sandoz Mescaline; Damian's Tale; The Black Jaguar; and Script for the Lost Reflection.

The Harvard Review: Beeches.

Inertia: An Ecclesiastical Sketchbook; Backstreets; Little Sur.

The Kenyon Review: Late Oracle Sonnet; The Auroras ("The Aurora Called Destiny"; "The Swan"; "The Aurora of the Midnight Ink"); In Bangkok.

Literary Imagination: Hungry Ghost; Creque Alley; The Empty Frame.

The Los Angeles Review of Books: To a Story.

The New Yorker: Iris; Dolls; Gin; Hush; The Shore; Blue Waves; Guitar; Hotel Sierra; Until the Sea Is Dead; Desire; The Reef; Shadow; The Swan at Sheffield Park; Leap of Faith; Without Mercy, the Rains Continued.

The Paris Review: *The Park*.

Poetry: The Avenues; Elegy; The Boathouse; Woman & Leopard; Rhapsody; In the High Country; From a Bridge; The Last Troubadour.

RUNES: Gypsy Davy's Flute of Rain.

The Southern Review: The Aurora of the New Mind; The Aurora of the Lost Dulcimer; Where He Came Down; The Way It Is; When My Baby Rocks the Funk; The One Who Should Write My Elegy Is Dead; Vineyard; Lucky; Generation; Equivalents; Emanations.

Spillway: Evangeline & Her Sisters; *The Stones of Venice*.

Tin House: Above Sunset.

The Yale Review: Chevalier d'Or.

"The Aurora of the New Mind" also appeared in *The Best American Poetry of 2008*.

"Elegy" also appeared in *The Pushcart Prize IV (1979)*.

"Emanations" also appeared in *The Best American Poetry of 2017.*

"Last Night with Rafaella" also appeared in *The Best American Poetry of 1990.*

"Late Oracle Sonnet" also appeared in *The Pushcart Prize XXXVIII (2014)*.

"Lucifer in Starlight" also appeared in *The Best American Poetry of 1992.*

"Merlin" also appeared in *The Best American Poetry of 1991.*

"Vineyard" also appeared in *The Best American Poetry of 2016.*

To Daniel Halpern, Terry Karten, Jessica Faust, and Susan Terris: endless thanks for their longtime editorial support.

To my children: David, Andrew, and Vivienne, and to Anna Journey, love everlasting.

I.

SELECTED POEMS

(1976–2012)

SLOW DANCE

It's like the riddle Tolstoy
Put to his son, pacing off the long fields
Deepening in ice. Or the little song
Of Anna's heels, knocking
Through the cold ballroom. It's the relief
A rain enters in a diary, left open under the sky.
The night releases
Its stars, & the birds the new morning. It is an act of grace
& disgust. A gesture of light:
The lamp turned low in the window, the harvest
Fire across the far warp of the land. The somber
Cadence of boots returns. A village
Pocked with soldiers, the dishes rattling in the cupboard
As an old serving woman carries a huge, silver spoon
Into the room & as she polishes she holds it just
So in the light, & the fat
Of her jowls
Goes taut in the reflection. It's what shapes
The sag of those cheeks, & has
Nothing to do with death though it is as simple, & insistent.
Like a coat too tight at the shoulders, or a bedroom
Weary of its single guest. At last, a body
Is spent by sleep: A dream stealing the arms, the legs.
A lover who has left you
Walking constantly away, beyond that stand
Of bare, autumnal trees: Vague, & loose. Yet, it's only
The dirt that consoles the root. You must begin
Again to move, towards the icy sill. A small
Girl behind a hedge of snow
Working a stick puppet so furiously the passersby bump

Into one another, watching the stiff arms
Fling out to either side, & the nervous goose step, the dances
Going on, & on
Though the girl is growing cold in her thin coat & silver
Leotard. She lays her cheek to the frozen bank
& lets the puppet sprawl upon her,
Across her face, & a single man is left twirling very
Slowly, until the street
Is empty of everything but snow. The snow
Falling, & the puppet. *That girl.* You close the window,
& for the night's affair slip on the gloves
Sewn of the delicate
Hides of mice. They are like the redemption
Of a drastic weather: Your boat
Put out too soon to sea,
Come back. Like the last testimony, & trace of desire. Or,
How your blouse considers your breasts,
How your lips preface your tongue, & how a man
Assigns a silence to his words. We know lovers who quarrel
At a party stay in the cool trajectory
Of the other's glance,
Spinning through pockets of conversation, sliding in & out
Of the little gaps between us all until they brush or stand at last
Back to back, & the one hooks
An ankle around the other's foot. Even the woman
Undressing to music on a stage & the man going home the longest
Way after a night of drinking remember
The brave lyric of a heel-&-toe. As we remember the young
Acolyte tipping
The flame to the farthest candle & turning

To the congregation, twirling his gold & white satin
Skirts so that everyone can see his woolen socks & rough shoes
Thick as the hunter's boots that disappear & rise
Again in the tall rice
Of the marsh. The dogs, the heavy musk of duck. How the leaves
Introduce us to the tree. How the tree signals
The season, & we begin
Once more to move: Place to place. Hand
To smoother & more lovely hand. A slow dance. To get along.
You toss your corsage onto the waters turning
Under the fountain, & walk back
To the haze of men & women, the lazy amber & pink lanterns
Where you will wait for nothing more than the slight gesture
Of a hand, asking
For this slow dance, & another thick & breathless night.
Yet, you want none of it. Only, to return
To the countryside. The fields & long grasses:
The scent of your son's hair, & his face
Against your side,
As the cattle knock against the walls of the barn
Like the awkward dancers in this room
You must leave, knowing the leaving as the casual
& careful betrayal of what comes
Too easily, but not without its cost, like an old white
Wine out of its bottle, or the pages
Sliding from a worn hymnal. At home, you walk
With your son under your arm, asking of his day, & how
It went, & he begins the story
How he balanced on the sheer hem of a rock, to pick that shock
Of aster nodding in the vase, in the hall. You pull him closer

& turn your back to any other life. You want
Only the peace of walking in the first light of morning,
As the petals of ice bunch one
Upon another at the lip of the iron pump & soon a whole blossom
Hangs above the trough, a crowd of children teasing it
With sticks until the pale neck snaps, & flakes spray everyone,
& everyone simply dances away.

IRIS

Vivian St. John (1891–1974)

There is a train inside this iris:

You think I'm crazy, & like to say boyish
& outrageous things. No, there is

A train inside this iris.

It's a child's finger bearded in black banners.
A singe window like a child's nail,

A darkened porthole lit by the white, angular face

Of an old woman, or perhaps the boy beside her in the stuffy,
Hot compartment. Her hair is silver, & sweeps

Back off her forehead, onto her cold & bruised shoulders.

The prairies fail along Chicago. Past the five
Lakes. Into the black woods of her New York; & as I bend

Close above the iris, I see the train

Drive deep into the damp heart of its stem, & the gravel
Of the garden path

Cracks under my feet as I walk this long corridor

Of elms, arched
Like the ceiling of a French railway pier where a boy

With pale curls holding

A fresh iris is waving goodbye to a grandmother, gazing
A long time

Into the flower, as if he were looking some great

Distance, or down an empty garden path & he believes a man
Is walking toward him, working

Dull shears in one hand; & now believe me: The train

Is gone. The old woman is dead, & the boy. The iris curls,
On its stalk, in the shade

Of those elms: Where something like the icy & bitter fragrance

In the wake of a woman who's just swept past you on her way
Home

& you remain.

DOLLS

They are so like
Us, frozen in a bald passion
Or absent
Gaze, like the cows whose lashes
Sag beneath their frail sacks of ice.
Your eyes are white with fever, a long
Sickness. When you are asleep,
Dreaming of another country, the wheat's
Pale surface sliding
In the wind, you are walking in every breath
Away from me. I gave you a stone doll,
Its face a dry apple, wizened, yet untroubled.
It taught us the arrogance of silence,
How stone and God reward us, how dolls give us
Nothing. Look at your cane,
Look how even the touch that wears it away
Draws up a shine, as the handle
Gives to the hand. As a girl, you boiled
Your dolls, to keep them clean, presentable;
You'd stir them in enormous pots,
As the arms and legs bent to those incredible
Postures you preferred, not that ordinary, human
Pose. How would you like me?—
Leaning back, reading aloud from a delirious
Book. Or sprawled across your bed,
As if I'd been tossed off a high building
Into the street,
A lesson from a young government to its people.
When you are asleep, walking the fields of another
Country, a series of shadows slowly falling

Away, marking a way,
The sky leaning like a curious girl above a new
Sister, your face a doll's deliberate
Ache of white, you walk along that grove of madness,
Where your mother waits. Hungry, very still.
When you are asleep, dreaming of another country,
This is the country.

GIN

There's a mystery
By the river, in one of the cabins
Shuttered with planks, its lock
Twisted; a bunch of magazines flipped open,
A body. A blanket stuffed with leaves
Or lengths of rope, an empty gin bottle.
Put down your newspaper. Look out
Beyond the bluffs, a coal barge is passing,
Its deck nearly
Level with the water, where it comes back riding
High. You start talking about nothing,
Or that famous party, where you went dressed
As a river. They listen,
The man beside you touching his odd face
In the countertop, the woman stirring tonic
In your glass. Down the bar the talk's divorce,
The docks, the nets
Filling with branches and sour fish. Listen,
I knew a woman who'd poke a hole in an egg, suck
It clean and fill the shell with gin,
Then walk around all day disgusting people
Until she was so drunk
The globe of gin broke in her hand. She'd stay
Alone at night on the boat, come back
Looking for another egg. That appeals to you, rocking
For hours carving at a hollow stone. Or finding
A trail by accident, walking the bluff's
Face. You know, your friends complain. They say
You give up only the vaguest news, and give a bakery
As your phone. Even your stories

Have no point, just lots of detail: The room
Was long and bright, small and close, angering Gaston;
They turned away to embrace him; She wore
The color out of season,
She wore hardly anything at all; Nobody died; Saturday.
These disguises of omission. Like forgetting
To say obtuse when you talk about the sun, leaving
Off the buttons as you're sewing up the coat. So,
People take the little
They know to make a marvelous stew;
Sometimes, it even resembles you. It's not so much
You cover your tracks, as that they bloom
In such false directions. This way friends who awaken
At night, beside you, awaken alone.

HUSH

for my son

The way a tired Chippewa woman
Who's lost a child gathers up black feathers,
Black quills & leaves
That she wraps & swaddles in a little bale, a shag
Cocoon she carries with her & speaks to always
As if it were the child,
Until she knows the soul has grown fat & clever,
That the child can find its own way at last;
Well, I go everywhere
Picking the dust out of the dust, scraping the breezes
Up off the floor, & gather them into a doll
Of you, to touch at the nape of the neck, to slip
Under my shirt like a rag—the way
Another man's wallet rides above his heart. As you
Cry out, as if calling to a father you conjure
In the paling light, the voice rises, instead, in me.
Nothing stops it, the crying. Not the clove of moon,
Not the woman raking my back with her words. Our letters
Close. Sometimes, you ask
About the world; sometimes, I answer back. Nights
Return you to me for a while, as sleep returns sleep
To a landscape ravaged
& familiar. The dark watermark of your absence, a hush.

THE SHORE

So the tide forgets, as morning
Grows too far delivered, as the bowls
Of rock and wood run dry.
What is left seems pearled and lit,
As those cases
Of the museum stood lit
With milk jade, rows of opaque vases
Streaked with orange and yellow smoke.
You found a lavender boat, a single
Figure poling upstream, baskets
Of pale fish wedged between his legs.
Today, the debris of winter
Stands stacked against the walls,
The coils of kelp lie scattered
Across the floor. The oil fire
Smokes. You turn down the lantern
Hung on its nail. Outside,
The boats aligned like sentinels.
Here beside the blue depot, walking
The pier, you can see the way
The shore
Approximates the dream, how distances
Repeat their deaths
Above these tables and panes of water—
As climbing the hills above
The harbor, up to the lupine drifting
Among the lichen-masked pines,
The night is pocked with lamps lit
On every boat offshore,
Galleries of floating stars. Below,

On its narrow tracks shelved
Into the cliff's face,
The train begins its slide down
To the warehouses by the harbor. Loaded
With diesel, coal, paychecks, whiskey,
Bedsheets, slabs of ice—for the fish,
For the men. You lean on my arm,
As once
I watched you lean at the window;
The bookstalls below stretched a mile
To the quay, the afternoon crowd
Picking over the novels and histories.
You walked out as you walked out last
Night, onto the stone porch. Dusk
Reddened the walls, the winds sliced
Off the reefs. The vines of the gourds
Shook on their lattice. You talked
About that night you stood
Behind the black pane of the French
Window, watching my father read some long
Passage
Of a famous voyager's book. You hated
That voice filling the room,
Its light. So tonight we make a soft
Parenthesis upon the sand's black bed.
In that dream we share, there is
One shore, where we look out upon nothing
And the sea our whole lives;
Until turning from those waves, we find
One shore, where we look out upon nothing

And the earth our whole lives.
Where what is left between shore and sky
Is traced in the vague wake of
(The stars, the sandpipers whistling)
What we forgive. *If you wake soon, wake me.*

BLUE WAVES

I think sometimes
I am afraid, walking out with you
Into the redwoods by the bay. Over
Cioppino in a fisherman's café, we
Talk about the past, the time
You left me nothing but your rugs;
How I went off to that cabin
High in the Pacific cliffs—overlooking
Coves, a driftwood beach, sea otters.
Some mornings, over coffee, we sit
And watch the sun break between factory
Smokestacks. It is cold,
Only the birds and diesels are starting
To sound. When we are alone
In this equation of pleasure and light,
The day waking, I remember more
Plainly those nights you left a husband,
And I a son. Still, as the clouds
Search their aqua and gray
Skies, I want only to watch you leaning
Back in the cane chair, the Navaho
Blanket slipping, the red falls
Of your hair rocking as you keep time
To the machinery gears, buses
Braking to a slide, a shudder of trains.
If I remember you framed by an
Open window, considering the coleus
You've drawn; or, with your four or five
Beliefs, stubborn and angry, shoving
Me out the door of the Chevy; or, if some

Day or night
You take that suitcase packed under
The bed and leave once again, I will look
Back across this room, as I look now, to you
Holding a thin flame to the furnace,
The gasp of heat rising as you rise;
To these mornings, islands—
The balance of the promise with what lasts.

THE AVENUES

Some nights when you're off
Painting in your studio above the laundromat,
I get bored about two or three A.M.
And go out walking down one of the avenues
Until I can see along some desolate side street
The glare of an all-night cafeteria.
I sit at the counter,
In front of those glass racks with the long,
Narrow mirrors tilted above them like every
French bedroom you've ever read
About. I stare at all those lonely pies,
Homely wedges lifted
From their moons. The charred crusts and limp
Meringues reflected so shamelessly—
Their shapely fruits and creams all spilling
From the flat pyramids, the isosceles spokes
Of dough. This late at night,
So few souls left
In the place, even the cheesecake
Looks a little blue. With my sour coffee,
I wander back out, past a sullen boy
In leather beneath the whining neon,
Along those streets we used to walk at night,
Those endless shops of spells: the love philtres
And lotions, 20th century voodoo. Once,
Over your bath, I poured
One called Mystery of the Spies,
Orange powders sizzling all around your hips.
Tonight, I'll drink alone as these streets haze

To a pale gray. I know you're out somewhere—
Walking the avenues, shadowboxing the rising
Smoke as the trucks leave their alleys and loading
Chutes—looking for breakfast, or a little peace.

GUITAR

I have always loved the word *guitar.*

I have no memories of my father on the patio
At dusk, strumming a Spanish tune,
Or my mother draped in that fawn wicker chair
Polishing her flute;
I have no memories of your song, distant Sister
Heart, of those steel strings sliding
All night through the speaker of the car radio
Between Tucumcari and Oklahoma City, Oklahoma.
Though I've never believed those stories
Of gypsy cascades, stolen horses, castanets,
And stars, of Airstream trailers and good fortune,
Though I never met Charlie Christian, though
I've danced the floors of cold longshoremen's halls,
Though I've waited with the overcoats at the rear
Of concerts for lute, mandolin, and two guitars—
More than the music I love scaling its woven
Stairways, more than the swirling chocolate of wood

I have always loved the word *guitar.*

ELEGY

If there is any dwelling place
            for the spirits of the just;
if, as the wise believe, noble souls
            do not perish with the body,
rest thou in peace . . .

—TACITUS

Who keeps the owl's breath? Whose eyes desire?
Why do the stars rhyme? Where does
The flush cargo sail? Why does the daybook close?

So sleep and do not sleep.

The opaque stroke lost across the mirror,
The clamp turned.
The polished nails begin the curl into your palms.
The opal hammock of rain falls out of its cloud.

I name you, *Gloat-of-*
The-stalks, drowse-my-embers, old-lily-bum.
No matter how well a man sucks praise in the end
He sucks earth. Go ahead, step
Out into that promised, rasp gratitude of night.

Seeds and nerves. *Seeds*

And nerves. I'll be waiting for you, in some
Obscure and clarifying light;
I will say, Look, there is a ghost ice on the land.

If the page of marble bleeds in the yellow grass,
If the moon-charts glow useless and cold,
If the grains of the lamp outlast you, as they must—
As the tide of black gloss, the marls, and nectar rise

I will understand.

Here are my gifts: *smudges of bud*,
A blame of lime. Everything you remember crowds
Away. Stubble memory,
The wallpaper peeling its leaves. Fog. Fog
In the attic; this pod of black milk. Anymore,

Only a road like August approaches.

Sometimes the drawers of the earth close;
Sometimes our stories keep on and on. So listen—

Leave no address. Fold your clothes into a little
Island. Kiss the hinges goodbye. Sand the fire. Bitch
About *time*. Hymn away this reliquary fever.

How the sun stands crossing itself in the cut glass.

How the jonquils and bare orchards fill each morning
In mist. The branches in the distance stiffen,
Again. The city of stars pales.
In my fires the cinders rise like black angels;
The trunks of the olives twist once towards the world.

Once. I will walk out into the day.

THE BOATHOUSE

All the last lessons of fatigue,
Every passage naming its reprieve—
Also, the few
Commitments of the heart. I thought
I'd pass as smoothly as a hand passes
Over a globe of light
Hanging in some roadside bar,
Or over the earth on its pedestal of oak
In a library. I believed I'd take
What came, a life with no diary's
Hieroglyphics,
Only the crooked arc of the sun.
Now, even the way I sleep speaks habit;
My body slipping into the heat,
The crumpled beds. Every voice I hear
Within my own (*of the father,*
The mother) remains a saying so
Lost to its history. Look
How I treated the day,
Waking listlessly beyond the pale
Of those horizons scored along another
Subtle back. And so trust
Seeps only into the most concrete
And simple acts: the fox coat, the slap,
The gin smashed against the window. Maybe
Homer had it right. A man sails
The long way home. Now,
Every new morning-after lights
Those medleyed veins of white wisteria

Strung

Above the door; no alibis survive. Half

Of the boathouse has collapsed, the shingled

Roof sloughing off its tiles—as

Even the sea sings one octave in the past.

HOTEL SIERRA

The November air
Has curled the new leaves
Of the spider plant, strung
From an L-bent nail
Driven in the warp of the window
Frame. Maybe the woman down
At the desk has a few more opinions—
On the dying plant, or the high
Bruised clouds of the nearing storm,
Or the best road
Along the coast this time of year
To Oregon. This morning, after
You left to photograph
The tide pools at dawn, the waves
In their black-&-white
Froth, I scavenged in your bag
For books, then picked up one
You'd thrown onto the bed, Cocteau,
Your place marked with a snapshot
Of a whale leaping clear of the spray
Tossed by the migrating
Herd—a totem
Of what you've left to dream. Yet,
It's why we've come—Hotel Sierra—
To this place without a past for us,
Where, I admit, a dozen years ago
I stayed a night across
The hall. I never asked why, on this
Ocean, a hotel was named for mountains
Miles inland. I spent that cold

Evening playing pinball in some dank
Arcade. Tonight, I'll take you there,
Down by the marina with no sailboats,
By the cannery's half-dozing, crippled
Piers rocking in the high tides and winds
Where I sat out on the rotted boards,
The fog barely sifting down,
The few lights
Looped over those thin, uneasy poles
Throbbing as the current came and went.
Soon, I could see only two mast lights
Blinking more and more faintly
Towards the horizon. I took
A flask of gin upstairs, just to sit
At the narrow window drinking
Until those low-slung, purposeful
Boats returned. As I
Wait here this morning, for you,
For some fragment of a final scene,
I remember how I made you touch, last
Night in the dark, those
Summer moths embossed upon the faded,
Imperial wallpaper of the room.
Now, as I watch you coming up
The brick-and-stone path to the hotel,
I can hear those loose wood shutters
Of the roof straining in the winds
As the storm closes
Over the shore. I listen as you climb
The stairs, the Nikon buzzing

Like a smoked hive
Each moment as you stop in front of:
A stairstep; a knob of the banister;
The worn brass "12" nailed
To our door; the ribbons: knots of paint
Peeling off the hall—
You knock open the door with one boot,
Poised, clicking off shot after
Shot as you slide into the cluttered room,
Pivoting: *me; the dull seascape hung*
Above the bed; the Bible I'd tossed
Into the sink; my hands curled on
The chair's arm; the limp spider plant. . . .
Next week, as you step out
Of the darkroom with the glossy proofs,
Those strips of tiny tableaux, the day
And we
Will have become only a few gestures
Placed out of time. But now rain
Slants beyond a black sky, the windows
Tint, opaque with reflected light;
Yet no memory is stilled, held frame
By frame, of this burlesque of you
Undressing. The odd pirouette
As your sweater comes off, at last,
Rain-soaked slacks collapsing on the floor.
Tomorrow, after we leave for good
The long story we've told of each other
So many years not a friend believes it,
After we drive along the shore to Albion

To your cabin set high above the road,
After we drag your suitcases and few boxes
Up to the redwood porch,
After the list of goodbyes and refusals ends,
We'll have nothing to promise. Before I go,
You'll describe for me again those sleek
Whales you love, the way they arc elegantly
Through water or your dreams. How, like
Us, they must travel in their own time,
Drawn simply by the seasons, by their lives.

SONG WITHOUT FORGIVENESS

You should have known. The moon
Is very slender in that city. If those
Letters I sent,
Later, filled with details of place
Or weather, specific friends, lies, hotels—
It is because I took the attitudes of
Shadow for solitude. It is because you swore
Faith stands upon a black or white square,
That the next move
Is both logical and fixed. Now, no shade
Of memory wakes where the hand upon a breast
Describes the arc of a song without forgiveness.
Everything is left for you. After the bitter
Fields you walk grow deep with sweet weeds, as
Everything you love loves nothing yet,
You will remember, days, you should have known.

UNTIL THE SEA IS DEAD

What the night prepares,
Day gives: this cool
Green weave to the light
Shading the darker emeralds
Of each branch as they descend
The narrow trunks of pine
And Douglas fir along the steep
Uneven slope of the hill,
Its jagged sockets of rock
And sudden gullies. Every amber
Bridge light fades at dawn,
A few redwoods cluster
By the pitted highway
At each bend, and, beyond,
Those white hummocks rise shagged
With ice plant and wiry scrub
Half a mile or so
Before they flatten at the sea.
There the shore cuts like a thin
Sickle at the fields
Of black waves. On a rise above
These dunes, I watch the wild oats
Leaning with the wind, as I try
To imagine what I could
Write to you beyond these few
Details of a scene, or promises
You already know. Perhaps
I'll draw myself into the landscape,
To hold you closer to it

Than I could alone. Below, the dunes
Grow dark even in this harsh
A light: the sand burns
With the same erratic white
Within a negative held up
Against the sun. These dunes—
The Dunes of Abraham—were named
For the story of a Russian
Trader who stayed
To live in the hills above Fort Ross,
Long after his fur company
And its hundred soldiers sailed home
To Alaska. In the spring
His Spanish wife left him, leaving
Also the clothes and books brought
From Madrid, and her small son,
Almost two. Late one night, he took
The boy down to the dunes
And tied him against the bent
Skeleton of an overturned skiff;
In the moonlight, the child
Shone blue and flat, like the fresco
Of a cherub painted high
Across the dome of a cathedral ceiling.
The Russian took his curved fishing
Knife, then hooked
Its point into the skin below
His chin's cleft and yanked the blade
Along the fraying vein of his

Own windpipe. At dawn, a woman driving
A drag of timbers
From the mill down to the harbor
Found the boy, alive, his skin laced
By welts where the taut ropes
Webbed his body. In towns along
The coast, they said
It was a miracle the way God
Had turned the hand of Abraham away
From the son, against the father. Some
Nights, in the pockets of these dunes,
A gull or bat will sweep up
In an ashen light, startled by the whisk
Of my pants in the stiff grass;
I'll stop until the urgent flapping
Dies, until both the body
And its shadow enter the fog beginning
Its nightly burning of the shore.
As the horns sound, a beacon
From the jetty skims the vague sands
Of the reefs. From here,
I can see the husk of the DeSoto
Someone pushed, last summer, off the cliff.
If I'm tired, sometimes
I'll sit awhile in its backseat—
In the mixed scent of salt, dead mollusks,
Moldering leather, and rust. The rear axle
Caught on the last low rocks
Of the cliff, the hood nosed dead-on

Into the tentative waves of a high tide,
The odd angle of the car,
Make it seem at any moment the rocks
Might give way, sending me adrift.
And I know I'll bring you here,
If only to let you
Face those dreams you woke me from
One night as the shore broke; I want
You to stand *here*—
Or, if you're bored with me,
We can walk up to the Whalers Cove
Where a few old shacks are left
By a single room-sized cauldron
Blackened by its years
Of fires melting acres of fat,
A pot too huge for even the scavengers
To think of carting it away. A local
Fisherman told me it was here
The Russian and his wife
Traded those first hard vows
Made to last longer than a double
Lifetime. Some
Should know better than to promise
Time, or their bodies, even if
Trust lives first in the body
Before rising like an ether
Into the mind. Tonight, walking alone,
I'll walk out into the cold mists
Up to the circular groves

High above the cabin, where the wild
Peacocks primp by the meadows or cry
From their invisible balconies
In the trees, their screams
Those of a child. And
From a prospect
Higher still, where the trees
Begin to grow more sparse and the rocks
More bare, I can look down
Onto the whole of the small harbor,
The bridge lights swaying
Once again, the jetty warning lamps
Blinking along the tower of the unlit
Beacon. The dunes rise and fall
Like shadows of waves down to the bay.
If you had been beside me, sleepless
Or chilled by the sudden violence
Of the winds, maybe you'd have walked
Here with me, or come after
To see what kept me standing in the night—
You'd see nothing. Only, what
Dissolves: dark to dawn, shore to wave,
Wings to fog, a branch to light:
The vague design that doesn't come
From me, yet holds me
To it, just as you might, another time.
And just as the Russian paced here
Rehearsing these lines, looking
Down onto the cove and whalers' shacks

Where she waited drawing a black
Comb out of her hair, I'll
Say for both of us the small prayer
Sworn to live beyond the night:
Until the stars run to milk,
Until the earth divides, until these waves
No longer rake the headland sands,
Until the sea is dead. . . .

A HARD & NOBLE PATIENCE

There is a hard & noble patience
I admire in my friends who are dead
Though I admit there are none of them
I would change places with

For one thing look how poorly they dress

Only one is still beautiful
& that is because
She chose to drown herself in a Swiss lake
Fed by a glacier said in local myth
To be a pool of the gods

& when her body was found she was so
Preserved by the icy currents
That even her eyelashes seemed to quiver
Beneath my breath

Though that was only for an instant

Before she was strapped to the canvas stretcher
& loaded into a blue van
Soon I was the only person still standing
At the lake's edge   A man made lonely
By such beauty

A man with less than perfect faith in any God

THE DAY OF THE SENTRY

Misery et cetera
Likely as the quilt of leaves
Above this confused congruence of
Sentience

If there were only one path leading away

From the small iron shed
Beside the glass summerhouse where
She sleeps like the broken string of a lute
Like the last in a series of broken
Strings

I might follow that path to the edge
Of the white lake the radical lake rising
All by itself into the air

Where a single cloud descended like a hand

Once while we sat watching
As the moon paced the hard horizon like a sentry
Whose borders had only recently begun
To assemble
Whose latitudes resemble a doubled thread
Whose path remains a sentence on the sleepy tongue

& in that mist of intersection
Lake cloud & moon combining in the slash
Of the instant

I had only the physical to remember you by

Only the heat of your breath along my shoulder
Only the lit web of wet hair streaking
Our faces like the veins of
No other night

No other
Now in the regrettable glare of the mind

Which worships our impermanence
The way in which you have become the *she* asleep
In the summerhouse
                    where the glass walls
Hold only the gold of the day's light

As if you never had any body I knew at all

DESIRE

There is a small wrought-iron balcony . . .
& at that balcony she stood a moment
Watching a summer fog
Swirl off the river in huge
Drifting pockets as the streetlights grew
Alternately muted then wild then to a blurred
Relay of yellow

Her hair was so blond that from a distance
It shone white as spun silk
& as he turned the corner he stopped suddenly
Looking up at the window of the hotel room
Where she stood in her Japanese kimono
Printed with red dragonflies
& a simple bridge

& in that lapse of breath
As the fog both offered & erased her in the night
He could remember every pulse of her tongue
Every pared detail of constancy left
Only to them   as he began
Walking slowly toward the door of the hotel
Carrying the hard loaf of day-old bread
& plums wrapped in newspaper

Already remembering this past he would desire

THE REEF

The most graceful of misunderstandings
I could not keep close at hand
She paused a moment
At the door as she adjusted her scarf against
The winds & sprays & in the moonlight
She rowed back across the inlet to the shore

I sat alone above my pale vodka
Watching its smoky trails of peppercorns
Rising toward my lips

& while I flicked the radio dial
Trying to pick up the Cuban station or even
The static of "The Reggae Rooster" from Jamaica

I watched the waves foam above the coral & recede

Then foam breathlessly again & again
As a school of yellowtail
Rose together to the surface & then suddenly dove
Touched I knew by the long silver glove

Of the barracuda she loved to watch each afternoon
As she let the boat drift in its endlessly

Widening & broken arc

WOMAN & LEOPARD

Jardin des Plantes; the zoo

Although she was beautiful,
Although her black hair, clipped
Just at the shoulders, glistened
Like obsidian as she moved
With that same slow combination
Of muscles as a dancer stepping
Casually beyond the spotlight
Into the staged, smoky
Blue of the shadows, it was
None of this that bothered me,
That made me follow her as she
Walked with her friends—a couple
Her age—along the wide dirt path
Leading to the island, the circle
Of cages where the cats glared
And paced. She was wearing a leather
Jacket, a simple jacket, cut narrowly
At the waist and dyed a green
I'd always coveted both in
Nature and out. It was the green of
Decay, of earth, of bronze covered by
The fine silt of the city, the green
Of mulch, of vines at the point
Of the most remote depth
In one of Rousseau's familiar jungles;
It was that jacket I was following—
Its epaulettes were torn at the shoulders;
The back was crossed by swatches
Of paler, worn horizons

Rubbed away by the backs of chairs;
Along the arms, the scars of cigarettes
And knives, barbed wire . . .
I think it was she who nailed that poster
To the wall of my small room in
The Hôtel des Grandes Écoles, an ancient photo
Of the Communards marching in a phalanx
Toward the photographer, tools
And sticks the poor
Weapons held ready in their hands.
It was a poster left up by every
Student or transient spending a night
Or week in that for-real garret,
Its one window opening out
Onto the roof, letting in both
The sunlight and winter rains, the drops
Or streams from the laundry hung to dry
At the window ledge, all of it
Running down along the poster, leaving
Streaks as ochre as the rivers crossing
The map of Europe pinned to the opposite
Wall. On the poster, faded by
Every year, those at the edge of the march
Had grown more and more ghostly, slowly
Evaporating into the sepia: half men,
Half women, half shadow. And I think
It was she in that leather jacket closing
The door to this room in May 1968 to march
With all the other students to the Renault
Factory, to plead again for some

Last unity. Those scars along the arms
Were neatly sutured in that heavy
Coarse thread that sailors use, a thread
Of the same fecund green. The woman,
Thirty-five perhaps, no more, glanced
At me; I watched
As she moved off away from her friends,
Over to the waist-high, horizontal
Steel rail at the front of the leopard's
Cage. I moved to one side, to see both
Her face and the face
Of the leopard she'd chosen to watch;
She began to lock it into her precise,
Cool stare. The leopard sat on
A pillar of rock
Standing between the high metal walkway
At the rear of the cage, where its mate
Strolled lackadaisically, and—below
The leopard—a small pond that stretched
Almost to the cage's front, a pool
Striped blue-&-black by the thin shadows
Of the bars. The woman stood
Very quietly, leaning forward against
The cold steel of the restraint, the rail
Pressing against the bones
Of her hips,
Her hands balled in the pockets
Of her jacket. She kept her eyes on the eyes
Of the leopard . . . ignoring the chatter of
Her friends, of the monkeys, of the macaws.

She cared just for the leopard,
The leopard tensing and arching his back
As each fork of bone pushed up
Along its spine—just
For the leopard
Working its claws along its high perch
Of stone, its liquid jade eyes
Dilating, flashing only for an instant
As the woman suddenly laughed,
And it leapt.

SHADOW

I am the shadow you once blessed

Though I was told later you meant only
To bless a small monkey carved of ebony
On the leg of a particular chair

Didn't you notice
That when you fell to your knees I too
Fell & kissed this scarlet earth

Blackened by the lyre of your wings

MERIDIAN

The day seemed suddenly to give to black-&-white
The falcon tearing at the glove
Clare yanking down the hood over its banked eyes
& handing the bird
Its body still rippling & shuddering & flecked
Here or there with blood
                              to her son Louis
& as we walked back up the overgrown stone trail
To the castle now in the public trust
For tax reasons she admitted
Supposing one more turn in the grave couldn't harm
Her father the Count much at this point anyway
Though she flew his favorite red flag
From one of the towers every year
To mark the anniversary of his death
& though her beauty had acquired the sunken
Sheen of a ship's figurehead lifted
From the clear Mediterranean
As she walked ahead of me in her high chocolate boots
I could think only of her body still muscled like a
Snake's & how she lay sprawled last night
Naked on the blue tiles of the bathroom floor
& as I stepped into the doorway
I could see the bathtub speckled with vomit
The syringe still hanging limply from a vein in her
Thigh & she was swearing
As she grasped for the glass vial
That had rolled out of reach behind the toilet
Then she had it
Drawing herself up slowly as she

Turned her body slightly to look up at me
& she said nothing
Simply waiting until I turned & walked away
The door closing with its soft collapse
Behind me
                  now over lunch on the terrace
I pin a small sprig of parsley to her jacket lapel
A kind of truce   a soldier's decoration
& above us the sun drags the day toward its meridian
Of heat & red wine & circumstance from which
We can neither look back nor step ever
Visibly beyond yet as we
Look at each other in the brash eclipsing glare
We know what bridging silence to respect
Now that neither of us has the heart to care

THE SWAN AT SHEFFIELD PARK

It is a dim April
Though perhaps no dimmer than any
London April my friend says
As we turn our backs
To the crooked Thames to the stark
London skyline
                      walking up the hill's
Mild slope to one of the paths
And prospects of Kew
He introduces
The various and gathered families
Of trees then every subtle
Shift of design along the grounds
The carefully laid views and pools
The chapel-sized orangery
Where citrus in their huge trolley tubs
Were wheeled behind the glass walls
And spared each winter
Fresh lime grapefruit and orange
That's what a queen wants
That's what the orangery says
Now April's skies grow a little
More forgiving
Breaking into these tall columns
Of white clouds
                      the kinds of elaborate
Shapes that children call God's Swans
Here in the country an hour
South of London
                      where Gibbon finished

Decline and Fall in Lord Sheffield's library
In the manor house I can see just there
In the trees
        as I walk with my friend along
The road that passes by his cottage
At the edge of the grounds of Sheffield Park
Once again
        the sky's high pillars collect
Into one flat unrelieved blanket
Above these shivering leaves
And bent blades
        a curtaining mist
Materializes out of the air
As we stop for a moment
On a stone bridge over the small falls
Between two of the lakes
And from the center of one of the lakes
A single swan glides toward us
Its wake a perfect spreading V
Widening along the water
        as each arm
Of the V begins to break against
The lake's shores
        the swan holds its head
And neck in a classical question mark
The crook of an old man's
Walking stick its eyes fixed on us
As it spreads its wings
In this exact feathery symmetry

Though it does not fly
                    simply lifting
Its head until the orange beak
Almost touches the apex of the stone
Arch of the bridge
Waiting for whatever crumbs we might
Have thought to bring
For a swan
              that now turns from us
Gliding with those same effortless gestures
Away without a glance back over
Its smooth shoulder
                    the mist
Thickens as the clouds drop lower
And the rain threading the branches and leaves
Grows darker and more dense
Until I can barely see the swan on the water
Moving slowly as smoke through this haze
Covering the surface of the lake
That white smudge sailing
To whatever shelter it can find and as
I look again there's nothing
                        only
The rain pocking the empty table
Of the lake
              so even the swan knows
Better than I to get out of the rain
The way it curled white as breath and rose
To nothing along the wind

                              tonight
By the wood stove of the cottage
Drinking and talking with my friend
I'll tell him about the two women
I saw last week in Chelsea
One of them wrapped in a jumpsuit of wet
Black plastic
                    her hair coal
Black greased and twirled into spikes
That fell like fingers onto her shoulders
But more alarming
                              those lines she'd drawn
Out from her mouth with an eyebrow pencil
Along her pale cheeks the perfect
Curved whiskers of a cat
And the other one
                    her friend dressed
In white canvas painter's pants white leather
Boots and a cellophane blouse
                              who'd dyed
Her hair utterly white then teased it
So that it rose
Or fell in the breeze lightly and stiffly
As feathers who'd painted her mouth
The same hard rubbery orange as a swan's
And even to a person of no great humor
Or imagination they were
                              these two
In the silent path they cut in the air
Along King's Road in every way

52

Beautiful
   and for the rest
Of the day I was so shaken I made
Myself stop for a drink in Soho
A strip joint called *The Blade*
I'd stumbled into and judging from my
Welcome not a place for the delicate
But I stuck it out through enough Scotch
To make me drunk fearless
And screaming through the first show
When at its end the final stripper
Stepped from the small stage right onto the bar top
Everyone clearing away the glasses and bottles
From the polished copper in front of them
As she threw off everything strutting
Down the narrow bar except
A white boa G-string
Shivering against her thighs as she
Kicked her silver high heels to either side
Then lay down in front of me
Her bare back and shoulders pressed flat
To the copper as it steamed and smudged beneath
Her body's heat
    the catcalls and hollers
Rising as she lifted each leg
Pointing her toes to the spotlights scattered
Across the ceiling
    her legs held in a pale V
The silver sequins of her high heels
Glittering in the lights but

Then she stood abruptly
And stepped back onto the stage not
Waiting a moment before turning her back
To the hoarse cheers
                        disappearing
In the sheer misty gauze of the old curtains
And as the lights came up there was
Where she'd been
Just the trails and webs of cigarette smoke
Those long curlicues in a tattoo of light
Those ghosts and feathers of dust
Still drifting down onto the bare tables
The glistening bar
                        onto the empty veiled stage
Of wood warped gently as waves

THE MAN IN THE YELLOW GLOVES

"They were kept in a wooden trunk
In one corner of the attic
A trunk my grandfather had painted
With red and black enamels
In the manner of the Chinese cabinets
He loved and could not afford
And inside the trunk the small box
Lined with a violet velvet
Where he kept his gloves
                              a box
That I believe should have held
A strand of pearls or a set
Of bone-handled
Carving knives from Geneva
A box fluted with ivory
And engraved with my grandfather's
Initials each letter
Still faintly visible in its flourish
Of script across the tiny brass shield
Holding the latch
                        one night
My mother dragged it out to remind
Herself of a particular
Summer at the lake when her father
Dressed to the teeth for once
In his life arrived at
The lakeshore for a cocktail party
At a neighbor's boat and stepped
Right off into the water

Trying to stretch the short distance
From the dock to the boat's deck
And though the water was extremely shallow
All anyone could see for a moment
Were his hands held barely
Up in the twilight up
Above the surface of the water
Not pleading for help not reaching for
A rope but simply keeping his gloves
Dry his gloves of lemon silk
Which he refused to let touch water
Or liquid of any kind but
He rose slowly in the foam
Walking up the muddy rocks kicking
And swearing
Making his way over to the lake's edge
His hands still held up as if
At gunpoint
To the applause of the whole
Party my mother said as she worked
The frozen clasp loose of its pin
And slid her fingernail along
The edge of the box
Where the mold held it
Until the thin lid peeled back
And inside
              the yellow silk
Lit against the violet lining
Each finger of each glove bent

Slightly in an undisturbed
Calm
The two thumbs folded
Precisely across the palms
As if to guard the long seams
Crossing each like a lifeline
And my mother held the two gloves
Up to the light to let us see
Their transparence
                              a glow
Like the wings of a flying fish
As it clears the sea's surface
Then she laid them in my own
Cupped hands
Each as faintly moist as a breath
And as she smoothed them again
Along the velvet of their box
I imagined how I might someday pull
Them on in elegant company
Though even then the gloves were as small
As my hands
And so the next summer with my family
Camping near that familiar lake
I decided one night to find the old dock
Long since replaced by a new marina
I took the kerosene lamp
And walked to the main road
Then along its low curving shoulders
Until I came to the pitted asphalt lane

That once led to the dock
I picked my way slowly through the rubble
Through the brush and overgrown branches
The small globe of light thrown
By the lamp falling
Ahead of me along the path
Until I could see the brief glitter
And glare of the lake
Where the stars had escaped their clouds
And stood reflected
                    and where the road
Once swung gently toward the pier
The rocks now fell off twenty feet
In a sudden shelf and at its bottom
The dark planking of the dock began
I held the lamp in both hands
Pressing my back against
The slick dirt-and-stone face of the shelf
I slid carefully down working the heels
Of my boots into the crags and juts
To slow myself in the clatter
Of twigs and gravel old
Paving rotted boards and bark
Until I stopped and caught my breath
Looking out over the old dock
The soft planks at my feet stretching
Past the water's edge
Held up still by a few fat pilings
And as I took the first

Of a few steps
                the moldered boards
Sagged and snapped beneath me splinters
Shooting up as I tried to leap clear
As one ankle twisted in the broken planks
And I fell face down onto the mossy
Dock the lamp
I'd been holding the whole time
Smashing in my hands the kerosene
Washing over the boards and my fingers
Up past both wrists and blazing
In a sudden and brilliant gasp of flame
I held up my burning hands
Yanking my leg up through the shattered boards
Rolling then falling onto the rocks below
My hands still aflame each a flat
Candle boned with five wicks
And then I remember only
The hospital in the village
Then the hospital in the city where
I lay for weeks
My hands bandaged and rebandaged
Like heavy wooden spoons
And beneath the crisp daily
Gauze the skin of each hand was seared
And blistered each finger raw
The pores dilating as the burnt skin
Was first bared to the air then to
The ointments

And each day more morphine
As the fever rose up my arms into
My mind my dreams until the morphine
Dimmed the nights and days
Until at last even I could stand to look
At the gnarled and shrunken hands
As if some child had made
The skeletons of wire
Then wrapped each poorly in doughy strings
Of papier-mâché
                    in the next year
My hands were stitched in a patchwork
Of dime-sized pieces of skin cut
And lifted from the small
Of my back or my legs
Until they began to resemble
Hands you might hold in your own
But since then and in the hottest
Weather it doesn't matter I've
Always worn these gloves
Not from any
Vanity but to spare myself and you
The casual looking away
These gloves of kid leather tanned
Soft as skin and dyed at my request
A pale yellow
                    the yellow of a winter lemon
In honor of my grandfather in honor
Of the fire as it dies

And if some men choose to walk
Miles in the country just
To look across the patches and divides
Of the landscape
Into the hills lakes and valleys
Or the dense levels of tree and cloud
So that they might better meditate upon
Their world their bitterness fatigue
Themselves well
I have only to take off one glove
Or another to stare down into the landscape
Of each scorched stitched hand
At the melted webs of flesh at the base
Of each finger
     the depressions
Or small mounts and lumps of scar
The barely covered bone
       or the palms
Burnt clean of any future any
Mystery so I'll pull back on
My gloves these
That I order each year from London
And if in the course of a dinner somewhere
I hear comments about the arrogance
Of a man who'd wear his gloves
Through an entire meal what a dandy
What an out-of-date mannered sort of parody
Of a gentleman
    I will not mind

If the mild shock and disapproval rise
When I wear my yellow gloves
I'll never pull one off to startle
Or shame everyone into silence
                              instead
I'll simply check to see that each glove
Is properly secure
                    that each pearl button
Is snugly choked in its taut loop
Its minute noose of leather"

LEAP OF FAITH

No less fabulous than the carved marble inner
Ear of a lost Michelangelo & more
Blinding than the multiple courts & interior facets
Of a black diamond held up in broken moonlight

This final geography acknowledges its trunks of
Ebony & its boughs of summer rain

Though there at the gate where Dante burned his
Initials into the face of the oak shield
I hesitated before following the switchback trail up
To the precipice overlooking the canyon the abyss
So relished by philosophy & when I saw you
On the opposite cliff in your long cape & gold
Shoes with frayed thin ribbons snaking up your ankles

Like anyone approaching from the foot of a bridge
I simply stepped toward you & below the bones
Of the fallen shone in the lightning & the prayers

& certainly it was there in that country
Braced between twin brackets of stone I saw only one
Belief remains for a man whose life is spared by

A faith more insupportable than air

TERRACES OF RAIN

And the mole crept along the garden,
And moonlight stroked the young buds of
The lemon trees, and they walked the five lands . . .
Sheer terraces, rocks rising
Straight up from the sea; the strung vines
Of the grapes, the upraised hands of the olives,
Presided and blessed. Between Vernazza
And Monterosso, along a path
Cut into the sea cliff, a place for lovers
To look down and consider their love,
They climbed up to the double-backed lane
Where a few old women gathered herbs
By the roadside. Voices—
Scattered in the hills above—
Fell like rushes in a wind, their rasp and echo
Traveling down and forever in the clear sea air . . .
Then clouds, then mist, then a universal gray . . .
Where Signore and Signora Bianchini are having lunch,
She stops to talk with them, weather being
The unavoidable topic. Slips of rain, a child's
Scrawl, sudden layers and pages—then, at last,
The fan of sunlight scraping clean
The sky. Here, the world's
Very old, very stubborn, and proud. In the twilight:
Shadow and other, watching the painted foam of
Waves running from the sunset
To the coves, the overturned skiffs, the white nets
Drying in the reddening air. She stood
Behind him, resting her hand on his shoulder. Night
Spread above them like a circling breeze,

The way a simple memory had once
Returned to Montale, calming his childhood
And a troubled winter sea. The air still cleansing,
She said, the heart that was uncleansable. The unforgiving
One, that heart. . . . A boy in an emerald sweater
Passed, out walking a mongrel in good spirits. Across
The scallop of bay, the boats began
Returning to the harbor. Silent. Harsh. Such country
Breaks the selfish heart. There is no original sin:
To be in love is to be granted the only grace
Of all women and all men.

(The Cinque Terre)

LAST NIGHT WITH RAFAELLA

Last night, with Rafaella,

I sat at one of the outside tables
At Rosati watching the *ragazzi* on Vespas
Scream through the Piazza del Popolo

And talked again about changing my life,

Doing something meaningful—perhaps
Exploring a continent or discovering a vaccine,
Falling in love or over the white falls
Of a dramatic South American river!—
And Rafaella

Stroked the back of my wrist as I talked,

Smoothing the hairs until they lay as quietly
As wheat before the old authoritarian wind.

Rafaella had just returned from Milano
Where she'd supervised the Spring collection
Of a famous, even notorious, young designer—

A man whose name brought tears to the eyes
Of contessas, movie stars, and diplomats' wives
Along the Via Condotti or the Rue
Du Faubourg Saint-Honoré.

So I felt comfortable there, with Rafaella,
Discussing these many important things, I mean
The spiritual life, and my own
Long disenchantment with the ordinary world.

Comfortable because I knew she was a sophisticated,
Well-traveled woman, so impossible
To shock. A friend who'd
Often rub the opal on her finger so slowly

It made your mouth water,

The whole while telling you what it would be like
To feel her tongue addressing your ear.

And how could I not trust the advice
Of a woman who, with the ball of her exquisite thumb,
Carefully flared rouge along the white cheekbones
Of the most beautiful women in the world?

Last night, as we lay in the dark,
The windows of her bedroom open to the cypress,
To the stars, to the wind knocking at those stiff
Umbrella pines along her garden's edge,
I noticed as she turned slowly in the moonlight

A small tattoo just above her hip bone—

It was a dove in flight or an angel with its
Head tucked beneath its wing,

I couldn't tell in the shadows . . .

And as I kissed this new illumination of her body
Rafaella said, *Do you know how to tell a model?*
In fashion, they wear tattoos like singular beads
Along their hips,

but artists' models
Wear them like badges against the daily nakedness,
The way Celestine has above one nipple that
Minute yellow bee and above
The other an elaborate, cupped poppy . . .

I thought about this,
Pouring myself a little wine and listening
To the owls marking the distances, the geometries
Of the dark.
         Rafaella's skin was
Slightly damp as I ran my fingertip
Along each delicate winged ridge of her
Collarbone, running the harp length of ribs
Before circling the shy angel . . .

And slowly, as the stars
Shifted in their rack of black complexities above,

Along my shoulder, Rafaella's hair fell in coils,

Like the frayed silk of some ancient tapestry,
Like the spun cocoons of the Orient—
Like a fragile ladder

To some whole other level of the breath.

(Rome)

I KNOW

The definition of beauty is easy;
it is what leads to desperation.

—VALÉRY

I know the moon is troubling;

Its pale eloquence is always such a meddling,
Intrusive lie. I know the pearl sheen of the sheets
Remains the screen I'll draw back against the night;

I know all of those silences invented for me approximate
Those real silences I cannot lose to daylight . . .
I know the orchid smell of your skin

The way I know the blackened path to the marina,
When gathering clouds obscure the summer moon—
Just as I know the chambered heart where I begin.

I know too the lacquered jewel box, its obsidian patina;
The sexual trumpeting of the diving, sweeping loons . . .
I know the slow combinations of the night, & the glow

Of fireflies, deepening the shadows of all I do not know.

LUCIFER IN STARLIGHT

Tired of his dark dominion . . .

—GEORGE MEREDITH

It was something I'd overheard
One evening at a party; a man I liked enormously
      Saying to a mutual friend, a woman
Wearing a vest embroidered with scarlet and violet tulips
    That belled below each breast, "Well, I've always
Preferred Athens; Greece seems to me a country
      Of the day—Rome, I'm afraid, strikes me
As being a city of the night. . . ."
    Of course, I knew instantly just what he meant—
      Not simply because I love
Standing on the terrace of my apartment on a clear evening
    As the constellations pulse low in the Roman sky,
The whole mind of night that I know so well
      Shimmering in its elaborate webs of infinite,
Almost divine irony. No, and it wasn't only that Rome
    Was *my* city of the night, that it was here I'd chosen
      To live when I grew tired of my ancient life
As the Underground Man. And it wasn't that Rome's darkness
      Was of the kind that consoles so many
    Vacancies of the soul; my Rome, with its endless history
Of falls. . . . No, it was that this dark was the deep, sensual dark
    Of the dreamer; this dark was like the violet fur
Spread to reveal the illuminated nipples of
      The She-Wolf—all the sequins above in sequence,
The white buds lost in those fields of ever-deepening gentians,
    A dark like the polished back of a mirror,

The pool of the night scalloped and hanging
Above me, the inverted reflection of a last,

         Odd Narcissus. . . .

       One night my friend Nico came by
Close to three A.M.—As we drank a little wine, I could see
    The black of her pupils blown wide,
The spread ripples of the opiate night . . . And Nico
    Pulled herself close to me, her mouth almost
      Touching my mouth, as she sighed, "Look . . . ,"
And deep within the pupil of her left eye,
    Almost like the mirage of a ship's distant, hanging
      Lantern rocking with the waves,
I could see, at the most remote end of the receding,
    Circular hallway of her eye, there, at its doorway,
At the small aperture of the black telescope of the pupil,
      A tiny, dangling crucifix—
Silver, lit by the ragged shards of starlight, reflecting
    In her as quietly as pain, as simply as pain . . .
Some years later, I saw Nico onstage in New York, singing
    Inside loosed sheets of shattered light, a fluid
Kaleidoscope washing over her—the way any naked,
      Emerging Venus steps up along the scalloped lip
    Of her shell, innocent and raw as fate, slowly
Obscured by a florescence that reveals her simple, deadly
      Love of sexual sincerity . . .
    I didn't bother to say hello. I decided to remember
The way in Rome, out driving at night, she'd laugh as she let
    Her head fall back against the cracked, red leather
      Of my old Lancia's seats, the soft black wind

Fanning her pale, chalky hair out along its currents,
      Ivory waves of starlight breaking above us in the leaves;
The sad, lucent malevolence of the heavens, falling . . .
        Both of us racing silently as light. Nowhere,
Then forever . . .
               Into the mind of the Roman night.

MERLIN

Italo Calvino (1923–1985)

It was like a cave of snow, no . . .
More like that temple of frosted, milk-veined marble
        I came upon one evening in Selinunte,
Athena's white owl flying suddenly out of its open eaves.
       I saw the walls lined with slender black-spined
         Texts, rolled codices, heavy leather-bound volumes
Of the mysteries. Ancient masks of beaten copper and tin,
      All ornamented with rare feathers, scattered jewels.
His table was filled with meditative beakers, bubbling
        Here and there like clocks; the soldierly
Rows of slim vials were labeled in several foreign hands.
      Stacks of parchments, cosmological recipes, nature's
Wild equivalencies. A globe's golden armature of the earth,
        Its movable bones ringing a core of empty
      Space. High above the chair, a hanging Oriental scroll,
Like the origami of a crane unfolded, the Universe inked
        So blue it seemed almost ebony in daylight,
The stars and their courses plotted along its shallow folds
      In a luminous silver paint. On an ivory pole,
        His chameleon robe, draped casually, hieroglyphics
Passing over it as across a movie screen, odd formulas
      Projected endlessly—its elaborate layers of
Embroidery depicting impossible mathematical equations;
        Stitched along the hem, the lyrics
Of every song one hears the nightingale sing, as dusk falls
      On summer evenings. All of our stories so much
         Of the world they must be spoken by
A voice that rests beyond it . . . his voice, its ideal melody,

Its fragile elegance guiding our paper boats,
                              Our so slowly burning wings,
Towards any immanent imagination, our horizon's carved sunset,
                The last wisdoms of Avalon.

THE FIGURE YOU

The figure *you*
Remains the speculative whip of my aesthetic

As in the latest chapter I've been writing
Called "The Erotics of the Disembodied Self"

Although I suppose the figure
You still suppose yourself to be is nevertheless

& upon reflection nothing more than the presence
Of someone else's moon-stunned body

Held quietly against your own just like the air
Or any other absence by which we learn to mark

The passing of yet another impossibly forgiven
& long-punishable night

NIGHT

When Carole Laure stepped onto the black stage
At the Bobino, she got such a hand

That Lewis Furey, at the baby grand
Back in the shadows, had to grin. That image

Of her, singing in a single spotlight,
Hair rippling as she gave it a brief

Toss, just like in *Get Out Your Handkerchiefs*,
Made us feel the world would be all right.

Later, drinking Armagnac at Le Dôme,
Watching the late-night Easter week parade

Down Montparnasse, I thought I saw, in a jade
& mauve raincoat, Carole Laure—walking home

With Lewis Furey, in a group of friends . . .
All laughing, as if the night would never end.

RHAPSODY

In the dictionary of sapphires
Only the rain confesses its regrets.
Even the Venetian courtier asleep
At the end of the bed forgets

The naked jewels at his fingertips.
Still, in our own prosaic silence
Even a simple breath upon the ear
Is a kind of violence.

Then, beyond the facets of sex,
Level as moonlight, some lost aspect
Of solitude touches your shoulders,
Still bare & glistening with sweat,

The soft white of new ice & fragile as air;
& so I know I must take care.

CHEVALIER D'OR

Sometimes not even behind his back

His old friends called him the *chevalier d'or*
Not in kindness nor even humor but envy

& each morning as he stepped

From the ancient porcelain tub onto the freezing
Ochre & maroon Mexican tiles of the bathroom floor

He could see in the mist-veiled mirror

That hard wet helmet of golden hair
He'd worn for years like an aging French rock star

Yet at certain moments on particular evenings

When the light in some desolate nightclub in Nice
Fell just right a woman who was a stranger

Might say to him how much he reminded her

Of Johnny Hallyday & then his lips would glisten
In the smoky air & his eyes

Would blink their eloquent sadness into song

& everywhere in the world weary companionable women
Would arise & touch again the soft lute of their

Most ancient & trusted troubadour

STORIES

She told me only three stories
In the week before she died

The first about the child she'd lost
A boy just seven

A climbing accident that summer
She'd taken a cabin in the Pyrenees

& the second was not a story at all
But simply a description of the Alfa Romeo

Her husband's lover drove up
To the door of their house the day he left her

It was the color she said of a mustard field
& then she turned to me & held out a snapshot

She'd taken from the drawer of her bedside table
A photo of herself on an empty pier at twenty

Nude she recalled beneath her robe of copper orchids
Which required she insisted no explanation but instead

As she required of me just this song of simple mystery

RED WHEAT: MONTANA

There is a kind of weeping so inconsolable
It occasions only silence

Just as there is a kind of silence so horrible it requires weeping

Naked at the tall bedroom mirror she had shorn in piles
The magnificent red hair I had always loved

The blanket of curls I would pull over my body at night

A ragged field of red wheat clipped & bundled at harvest
& as I stood in the doorway she turned & said

Next week they said next week the treatments will "commence"

& in that pause I saw the sneer of a smile begin
As she said but today you & I will go & introduce ourselves

At Madame Récamier's Modern House of Wigs

BEECHES

The forest is its own thanksgiving
Walking a mile or so from the road
Past the lake & ancient post office
I skim the long bodies of the beech trees

The elegant ascension of their slender trunks
A kind of gorgeous illusory play
Of white bars against the dark ochre matting
Of the earth below

Peace is where you find it
As here the last secret of the dawn air mixes
With a nostalgia so perfumed by misery
Only the rhythm of the walk itself

Carries me beyond the past
To say I miss you is to say almost nothing
To say the forest is the sanctuary of ghosts
Is only the first step of my own giving way—

Not the giving up—just the old giving thanks

THE PARK

It was I think a small town in Ohio

I taped to the wall above my office desk the postcard
Of Klimt's painting called *The Park*

An example of cliché so profuse it touched my heart

Consoling me each time I turned my glance to its
Storm of tiny moth-sized leaves shimmering over all but the bottom

Ribbon of the canvas where the rows of the trunks individuate

The mass of the pulsing foliage above
A figure in a kimono or a robe so lush it too seems foliate

Stands apart from two other figures similarly dressed

But (the two) huddled closely together & moving off the sheer
Right edge of the canvas

& the solitary figure remains oddly hesitant & indistinct

& pensive although
Perhaps she is simply realizing that she does not wish to go

Where all of the others wish to go

THE RED LEAVES OF NIGHT

In my dream we are walking together

Through a forest of blanched birch & ragged beech perhaps
I know only that the trunks reflect their mottled

& luminous white bodies in the moonlight

& as we walk to some destination we seem not to know
I notice that the forest floor is matted again

With a blanket of fallen red leaves each as narrow as a finger

Thin pages torn from a pilgrim's book & some
Seem to have scrawled upon them sentences that themselves

Are written in the sticky red of blood entries

In the journal I heard you promise God you will burn tomorrow
& as we walk I can feel beneath my bare feet how soft

& cushioned by such fallenness this passage has become

This journey through the forest of the night
Along a path of red sorrows leading us together to some newly solitary

& distant home

THE AURORA OF THE NEW MIND

There had been rain throughout the province
Cypress & umbrella pines in a palsy of swirling mists
Bent against the onshore whipping winds

I had been so looking forward to your silence
What a pity it never arrived

The uniforms of arrogance had been delivered only
That morning to the new ambassador & his stable of lovers
The epaulettes alone would have made a lesser man weep

But I know my place & I know my business
& I know my own mind so it never occurred to me

To listen as you recited that litany of automatic miseries
Familiar to all victims of class warfare & loveless circumstance
By which I mean of course you & your kind

But I know my place & I know my business & baby
I know my own grieving summer mind

Still I look a lot like Scott Fitzgerald tonight with my tall
Tumbler of meander & bourbon & mint just clacking my ice
To the noise of the streetcar ratcheting up some surprise

I had been so looking forward to your silence
& what a pity it never arrived

Now those alpha waves of desire light up the horizon
Just the way my thoughts all blew wild-empty as you stood
In the doorway to leave   *in the doorway to leave*

Yet I know my place & I know my business & I know those
Melodies *melodies* & the music of my own mind

GYPSY DAVY'S FLUTE OF RAIN

Gypsy Davy came along
He sang so strange and sweetly

I'd filled the final page of my diary
A lovely thing given to me by the Lady of the Lake
& bound in a cover of tooled leather

The color of late-summer heather
& a single emerald spiking up at its center

To signal the green eye of the peacock carved there
So jealously guarding my words

Jealousy jealousy oh yes so much of what
I'd written in its pages only fable after fable
Of men always at odds with the truth

Men whose belief in love was so unequivocally
Selfish & provisional
The slightest little breeze off the hem of a skirt
Flowed along the river of their dreams & slowly

I learned my job was to play just a little tune

On a flute of jade & rain
To sing a simple song about the end of pain

& if you read on you'll no doubt discover those ways

Such strange tender renders new life to any
Woman or man who'd follow a song beyond the beds
Of the forgotten

                    into lavish fields of blue light

Only the luckiest lovers may claim

THE AURORA OF THE LOST DULCIMER

My favorite Appalachian dulcimer had suddenly left "on holiday"
But that wasn't going to stop me

I went to call on the ancient blues legend in his sixth-floor
Walk-up down on the Avenues because you know

I'd come too far to let the harsh estrangement of an instrument
Collude in such a singular disappointment

I was just like Ulysses but better dressed
Against the call of all the blue sirens lighting up Desire

& the moment my riverboat had docked along the fat pier
At New Orleans I'd set off on my mission

To step right off into that long-legged darkness with nothing
To protect me but my flaming Koa 1937 Nioma Hawaiian guitar

& the faith the songs that I knew were there awaiting me
Were the lessons I could paste like armor

Along the ragged seams of my soul those soul patches
For those soul scars & finally as I knocked on his worn door

I could hear the metal clasps of his guitar case
Snapping like the jaws of an alligator biting at summer flies

Then he opened up just standing there
In a purple bathrobe over a torn T-shirt & freshly pressed jeans

Smiling the way the moon smiles down on Lake Pontchartrain
& so began my true education & the resurrection of my good name

LATE ORACLE SONNET

1) Up late last night up late now this morning

2) *The new clover whitening the hillside*

3) The glass empty on the zinc counter

4) Also the white thimble of coffee awaiting you

5) *The cello she once painted turquoise & black*

6) Nobody cares nobody moves nobody thinks

7) *The spray of iris sprawled across the sofa*

8) The windows are blank with last night's rum

9) *The rhinestones suckled in the lead of the day*

10) The comfrey & the feldspar & the drying mud of night

11) *The columns made entirely of white dust*

12) That terrible taste that horrible taste

13) *The anise seeds lodged in the teeth of the corpse*

14) The opal ink scrolling the single page of her skin

IN THE HIGH COUNTRY

Some days I am happy to be no one
The shifting grasses

In the May winds are miraculous enough
As they ripple through the meadow of lupine

The field as iridescent as a Renaissance heaven
& do you see that boy with his arms raised

Like one of Raphael's angels held within
This hush & this pause & the sky's lapis expanse?

That boy is my son & I am his only father
Even when I am no one

FROM A BRIDGE

I saw my mother standing there below me
On the narrow bank just looking out over the river

Looking at something just beyond the taut middle rope
Of the braided swirling currents

Then she looked up quite suddenly to the far bank
Where the densely twined limbs of the cypress

Twisted violently toward the storm-struck sky
There are some things we know before we know

Also some things we wish we would not ever know
Even if as children we already knew   & so

Standing above her on that bridge that shuddered
Each time the river ripped at its wooden pilings

I knew I could never even fate willing ever
Get to her in time

WITHOUT MERCY, THE RAINS CONTINUED

There had been
A microphone hidden

Beneath the bed
Of course I didn't realize it

At the time & in fact
Didn't know for years

Until one day a standard
Khaki book mailer

Arrived & within it
An old

Stained cassette tape
Simply labeled in black marker

"Him / Me / September 1975"
& as I listened I knew something

Had been asked of me
Across the years & loneliness

To which I simply responded
With the same barely audible

Silence that I had chosen then

HUNGRY GHOST

When I came to see you
It hurt me how thin you had become

In the months of addiction & disease
& although your particular abyss

Was a man & not a drug
The degradation was the same

The same wasting of the flesh
The same tapped-out well emptied

Of the least leaf of emotion
The same frozen rage

When I came to your hotel room
You were sitting in a hard chair

Just by the window
Half-slumped & distracted

Looking out at the persistent rain
Then silently back at me

Your ghost your own ghost
Had already come

She sat by you at the small table
& she was so hungry

At one point she reached over
Reached right inside you

& slowly twisted off a moist
Wafer of your heart

She put it in her mouth
& let it sit a moment on her tongue

Her lips parting in a way both
Petulant & suggestive

It was clear she would eat
All of you

I walked into the bathroom
& at the dulled zinc sink

I rinsed one by one
The fat spring strawberries

I'd brought you from the ranch
I put them in the white

Ceramic bowl
I'd carried from our kitchen

& without a word simply placed it
On the table

Just beside your ghost
She stared at me & then only

At the fleshy rubies awaiting her
& ate until only a few

Rivulets of blood traced
The bottom of the bowl & the green

Crowns she'd torn from
Their bodies

Lay scattered where
They had fallen at her feet

At last she seemed sated
Placated or even bored

She barely looked over as
I wrapped you in your overcoat

You glanced at her
& she at you

The rain
Still steady at the pane

& then I realized you could
Not stand

Alone & so I lifted you up
To take you home

CREQUE ALLEY

For sixteen years or more
She said she'd slept only

With black men either African
Or Caribbean she'd picked up

In the reggae & zouk bars
In Creque Alley during her time

In San Francisco doing phone
Solicitation by day & sex trade

By night her blond hair by then
In exquisite cornrows down to

The middle of her back &
To break the cycle she admitted

Was killing her decided to
Marry one for the money & so

The green card he required
& another after he'd chained her

To the bed & kept her for weeks
Before she'd agreed & no

She didn't know where either of
Her husbands might be though

She now lived spitting distance
Of Point Lobos where one day

She'd stood far out on the rocks
As the tide came in & called me

On her cell saying listen to the surf
In which I am about to die

& I said No you're far too sick to die
& then she laughed & said please

Don't ever write about my illness
Which I despise though say

Anything you want about my father
Fucking me again & again

But please nothing of the way the virus
Has melted my body to bone

Then your horrible friends will know
All my life before you & diagnosis

I will claim again now as my own

RECKLESS WING

The window was open & a horse ran
Along the far edge of our field

You sat just opposite me
At our small kitchen table

& with one unbroken gesture
Swept your arm across its yellow

Formica clearing onto the floor
Coffee cups plates thatched with rinds

Of toast scarred by yolk newspapers
Notebooks & all of those distances

That'd gathered for months settling
Over everything & across this expanse

You raised your eyes to mine to make
Plain another new beginning

THE EMPTY FRAME

In the late spring or early
Summer of the year my family

Would drive past these fields
As we'd make our way in a black

Dodge up Tollhouse Road for
Shaver Lake or Huntington Lake—

Places my father often told me
He'd spent the best bar none

Summers of his life—yet in my
Own teens it was instead to these

Same foothills of the Sierras
I'd return always these meadows

Of long stiff marsh grass gone
Dry in the heat randomly stitched

By the spring wildflowers
& slow needles of piercing sunlight

I'd walk alone in those low hills
Or with the girl

I'd soon marry very soon to be also
The mother of our son

I need to tell you this now
Because I have you by me the one

I've waited for to sketch finally
The story of a boy who'd lie

At night in those fields believing
A world beyond always awaited

Restless in its insistent music
Now after the years of sickness

& lies I'm asking you in your
Stillness to hold this ledger of

Spring accounts & recall the plain
Mariposa lilies & the goldenrod

& the crowns of thistle & the yellow
Star-tulips & the clusters of wild clover

Dusted white & the faint musk mallow
& the endless waves of lupine

All blooming in a way I thought
Might hold me safely forever

& I need to tell you sometimes
I'd fall asleep out in those open fields

Always near the abandoned farm
I loved—its shaky one-room cottage

Still standing though by then releasing
Its boards to the steady season

Its crippled barn already long broken
To its knees & rotting & holy & yet

Wherever in the world I'd travel
It was the memory of that cottage

I'd carry with me I'm not sure why
Even so derelict & so many years

Abandoned it felt always somehow
Like home to me & last night at dusk

I drove again after these forty years out
Tollhouse Road along the long stretch

Leading past Academy & the cemetery
Where Ollie's family still presides

Then I pulled over at the familiar dirt
& gravel turnout where the same

Weathered planks & fence posts
Rose cracked & swiped by long grasses

Below the white limbs of that ancient oak
I walked out into the meadow

Leading to the old farm & though I saw
The cottage itself was finally gone

& only odd uneven squares of cracked
Foundation blocks still stood

Sinking into the long white grass
I could also see I swear to you just

Above & slightly to the right of the three
Concrete steps leading up to what

Now was nothing & no doorway
I could see hanging there impossibly

In the air exactly as it had always hung
Yet now only as the empty frame

Of the landscape nailed upon
The crossbeam of the blackening night

The same kitchen window that once
Opened onto these fields of wildflowers

& it floated precisely where it had
As if the cottage itself were yet standing

As if it were now my own window
& I could see that a light was burning

Once again within as if yes you were
Somehow waiting exactly

As I'd imagined these past months
Waiting at the burled black oak

Table with warped legs & its surface
Scarred by your bracelets & keys

Having your evening coffee over
A field guide of trails or alpine blossoms

& so I need now to ask you
Which of the old journals did you first

Open to a map of my long wandering
When did you first know I'd come back

& how did you find yourself here
& how did you know this single lantern

You are reading by was the last possible
Light to lead me home?

THE AURORAS

I. *Dawn Aurora*

The nothing you know is as immaculate a knowing
as any moment moving from a distance into dawn.
All of the awakenings, or the old unconscious lies . . .
I'd waited all night, holed up in Selene's derelict houseboat—
drinking tea, drinking Scotch, thinking of the rain
that night in Camden Town when she went missing for hours,
coming back only to say, Sayonara baby; thinking of
the way so many things touch their own fates. The motorcycle

heads for the cliff, or the bus stops just before the bench.
Everything seems more shabby in the dusk; everything glorious
holds its light. Look to your sons, look to your daughters.
Look to the blades rising out of the dark lawn. Don't worry;
each of your myths remains emblazoned upon the air. The way
the wind moves across the vellum of the mountain,
as the silence lifts its chords from the old piano. In the still dark
& still uncertain dawn, there begins that slow revelation larger

than the mind's, as the light grows coronal, & the house fills
with those elaborate agendas of the day. The monastery & philosophy
this morning, both seem so far away.

II. *Lago di Como*

The blood of the visible hangs like blossoms of bougainvillea
as they turn & twist along the lattice of limbs shading your
terrace, stretching like a ruby squid across one corner of the stone
villa above the lake. We sit looking out over the unqualified excellence
of the morning, & there is nothing you might desire to recall. You
believe in a space that is as large as logic, that is as logical as the word.

Tell me. What is the "beautiful," what is the "lost," & what lives still, just
at the edge of the sound of the trees? It could be the syllables of habit;
it could be a single phrase of gratitude . . . or an unbroken prayer. Tell me.
What will stay, & what will hold its grace & lasting ease?

III. *Autumn Aurora*

The illusionist steps to the stage. Everything
he claims will be, will be. I know because I've watched him
before the curtains began to part, & I've seen he is not just
one man, but he is also a woman. He is as multiple
as the rain. He is all children in the future—those children
both the woman & the man he is will bring from their couplings,
their embraces, & those silences of the clasped plural of their

nights, their individual nights. How have you left me? You have
left me with my hopes. How have you dreamed of me? You
have dreamed of me beneath the cool of the evening. There I am,
holding my dulcimer, holding my mandolin. There I am, singing
to you, always, singing to you, always, across the blade of time.
In the monograph of dawn, all of the tendencies of shifting light . . .
& now the bells are sounding. This evening, we will discover

only the fragrance of the October moon.

IV. *Florentine Aurora*

I saw what would proclaim itself as *beauty-beyond-surface*.
It was the rarest of days. I'd walked directly from the train station
& found the gallery empty, yet filled with a golden light as if dozens of
gilt bees rose lazily to the eaves, each a reflected particle of the afternoon.
It was a whole universe lifted by the painting; it was a universe
    that mirrored
the afternoon—& its singular burnishing within the painting—
    & the young
women, articulating the angles of desire, the hopeless erotic fortune
that proves itself in beauty. The shell of the day unfolding, the perfume of
the moment filling every pore we call the imagination. The day, today,
    seems
inexhaustible. This is my praise; this is my proclamation. This is the apple
I place on the white plate, before you. This is my metaphysics
    of possibility.
This is the fury of the present. This is the memory of the questions
I offer like pewter goblets. Let us share what remains, while it remains.

V. *The Aurora Called Destiny*

Selene was hearing voices again. It had become something
she was apt to do now & then; she heard the voices,
but she could not recall the names. . . . When she slept, voices
choired her into the heavens, & when she awoke they lay her
along the bed of dawn. She was precise & independent
in this illumination, & she found herself in the descent of many wings,

like a vortex of angelic understandings. Everything that seemed to sing
echoed in harmony around her, & the fevered happiness broke
like sweat along her skin. If the body shows it is the soft
white of wax, if the fox moves across the field & the white meadows
by the black woods, then what do we know of our deaths? What do we
know of the impossible weathers we must transcend?

What do we know of the milk
of the future & the milk of the end? Here is your destiny it is the color
of lapis & mirrors, of the glass which empties itself of time, of every
whisper. Here, at the oak dining table, place your palms upward facing, so
the sky can read the lines crossing there, & the grain of what remains.
This is not the epitaph you imagine. This is not some phantom

fear. Or else, I suppose, it is.

VI. *The Swan*

Nakedness only is never marriage, just as the pilgrim
looks beyond all fictive weavings of our oracles. In my notebook,
I keep my list of questions ready for the stranger at the crossroads:
How can I keep my life luminous, & how can I keep the day delivered?
Where does my constant taste for evasion end & the altar begin?
Where does the word become the Word, & why does the flesh
    remain flesh?

In the quiet of the park, the water spreads out before us, & the single
swan cuts across the water's blackness like a piece of music, like the fall
of an iris upon the table at dawn. Where have the minstrels gone, where
the loves that were lifted up in fables like the mantles of sorcerers
& the manes of their stallions, that white, white hair? I believe
the blank wall

remains blank for several lifetimes, & then finally there is the inked
    reason
of the figure. Look, the stranger's nails are lacquered silver, as she stands
at the roadside, white as light. There, with a feather boa & auras
    of the notice
we allow to be born of sexual repose, with the movement that becomes
    the very
fragrance of the vines, & all the pulses of afterward, & all the drowsy
refractions of her fatal, far-wingèd independence.

VII. *Ghost Aurora*

All of the apostles, the fortune-tellers, all of those committed
to the origins of reason or faith—each is now lost in the hum

of her or his own deepening meditation. What could be the purpose
of those songs the troubadour from Avignon brought us in his
   leather bag?

What could be the meaning of the carvings of green falcons along
the gourd-like back of his lute? What could be more useful than a loving

principle lifted slowly out of particles, like the frond of a morning fern
uncurling? Take up your coat; take up the morning. This is what it means

to lure the phantom out of the dark, until she lifts us into the space
   of song.

VIII. *Aurore Parisienne*

Selene became the pilot of her fate, dressed in careless breezes
& summer birds. Her sandals were stitched with fire & the summer moths
hovered at her toes. She shuffled in the chaos & she could not help,
     she said,
but drink the poison of her past, every mortal coil, every green core. All

those ancient probabilities echoed as she spoke, each in its own pastoral
     refrain,
like light lifted from a sepulcher, like the oblivion of the lamp & its
     cold globe
standing for the illumined but lost spirit. There, the abyss & the storm
& her desire all came to be one. If the forest beyond arose, it was
     the forest she
understood. Who else could move this way, except one already lost . . . as
     she said,

Think of me walking along the Seine, as I think of you in the twilight
     & the echo
of the day, lifting very slowly two ancient books before you . . . their
     songs arising still
even in the automatic flak of traffic, even as the swallows & martins
     slowly swirl.

IX. *Père Lachaise*

The names that have been unnamed arise, cold & clear
as the inscriptions upon the virgin stone. There, the rubies shone
against the onyx; there, those charnel house weathers, & the love
that must emerge like love. On the other side of the world, my
best friend dressed only in small brass cymbals. They were the size
of quarters & linked by either wire or cord. He had no idea what it
meant. He knew only as he moved each movement was announced by
the most glorious sound, chimes & rattles & an iridescence in the ear
the golden weather of himself shimmering everywhere. When they
found him later, dead, they said how pagan he'd become in his
    nakedness,

in his glory.

X. *The Book*

What is it about the motives of the night? All of those lovers
walking in the luster of their pasts. The strings of melody plucked
in the lightness of sleep.
                              What is it about the body
awakening beside you, rippling with that ultimate, jubilant fire?

Here in the strange, strange inn at the edge of the wood
there is the sacrifice of the leaves, all of the vestments abandoned.
All of the false stitching of the heraldry hanging, those banners of
death along the walls. I could not tell you, but there, outside,
the hinds hid & the hounds hung their heads, & it was in the room

above the inn, the raucous calamity of the inn, there by the bed,

She stood naked, clothed only in the knowledge of herself,
knowing the spider hanging in the corner between the raw beams
& the armoire was something as unofficial as the end—& there,
naked, redolent with the flames of the fire, with those embers
    rendering
light like language . . . she was, herself, a moving myth, self-announced

as any emblem of a life unfolding upon the air, the light, though
    the book
that she opened, the only book she knew, remained flat as a world,
    its pages

made luminous by the mind.

XI. *The Aurora of the Midnight Ink*

Will you really walk from one edge of the city to the other
dressed only in illusion & shame? How can I urge you to turn back?
Selene, when we return, we return to the book. The book opens,
& the world unfolds into its latticework of hymns. It is the excruciating
alchemy by which the spirit lives. I will live there with you, in the hotel
of the spirit, where the sheets are changed daily. Every instinct for

darkness is countered by yet another instinct for the light. Stand with me,

as I stand beside you in my jacket from Verona, its deep slate blue of
the gentlemen on their *passeggiata*. Here, take my pen, the scarred
   Montblanc
or the old Parker 50—it's your choice tonight—& write to me
in the script of the present, write to me about those long white petals of a
carpenter's shavings uncurling from his plane; write to me & tell me how
the mind can require such certainty of the dark. Any unfolding is an

unfolding into light, that unlocked origami of the light—the light slowly
lining again those faces, those facets, of our yet unfolding story.

XII. *Dark Aurora*

What a beautiful letter you wrote to me. It was as ripe
as a planet, & as much to the point. It was filled I saw not
with revelations or expectations. It was a space that expanded
like space. All I could do was respond with the poor reflex of intellect,
which is to say the insufficiency of a hedgehog & the modest vocabulary
of a saint. Darkness, darkness. What unfolds folds out away from us.

If death has a form, it is the form of departure. If death has a form,
it is lit by darkness. Everything we've looked for all these years,
everything together we've called some necessity of invention, any
syllable & symbol, every penetrating & luminous or prodigious desire,
every carved line on every page has emptied into this flesh, this flash
of revelation, this form which is no memory, which is our dark, the form

of dark, & darkness in its final form.

II.

THE WAY IT IS

(NEW POEMS)

WHERE HE CAME DOWN

In a field of weeds blowing behind a Texaco station
    in Cheyenne, Wyoming

In a hallway outside the door of his dealer's ex-wife where
    he knows she's hiding with her grandfather's Luger

On the pine-shadowed bank of the Merced River & beneath
    the blistering sunlight washing over Tuolumne
    Meadows

Watching the prairie falcons & minute pine siskins
    & the ending of someone's love

Or in the old apartment off North Avenue the blood-sketched
    floor scattered with strangers' works

Or in the one empty stall in the Plaza Hotel men's room before
    the awards ceremony begins   & lastly into

Those thin careful arms awaiting Icarus

HOT NIGHT IN AKRON

My downstairs neighbors were out for the night
    seeing the Clash in Cleveland

Which meant it was ok for Jolene to practice her
    flamenco routine on my linoleum

Kitchen floor in just Cuban heels & T-shirt having
    uncurled from the bed just a moment

Before & I still couldn't move even one muscle
    as the riveting gunshot rhythms

Began to ricochet through my little apartment
    but I rose up on one elbow

To answer the clanging of the phone on the floor
    right by the mattress & it was my

Once friend Elijah still way PTSD after five years
    in country & out & before I could try

Closing the bedroom door he asked *Are those shots?*
    as he heard the flamenco's crescendo

& I said Yeah but nothing serious just some assholes
    popping off at the frog pond

Then he started up telling me he didn't know where
    his wife was but when he did find out

He'd kill the motherfucker she was sleeping with
     & it went on like this a while before

I said Good luck & I had to go & just then Jolene stopped
     dead in her steps & peeled off her T-shirt

The sweat pouring off her as I walked over to wrap both
     arms around her & hold on a moment

Before I told her I guess you better go home now
     that was Elijah calling & she asked me

What did he want? & I said Just you

THE WAY IT IS

Tonight the hungry boys are out looking for all the hungry
      girls Delilah says & that's just the way it is

Just the way it's always been all those hungry girls all
      those hungry boys their naked ribs bright
      as vibraphones

Shined by the tracks of somebody's sweat & as I look back
      at those nights claws bared & bloody

I wish I could remember just one thing that tasted even a little
      like tenderness & of all the things I wanted

I never once meant to fool you into thinking I was simply
      your ordinary guy who just took a wrong turn

Somewhere on those streets dissolving sweet as lightning
      along the pitch & ink of summer sky

WHEN MY BABY ROCKS THE FUNK

When my baby rocks the funk & the night shakes its
    silky booty I go upstairs

& dig deep into my attic trunks to drag out those zebra
    bell-bottoms & snakeskin platform boots

So I can properly call down the vibrating Mothership
    & when my baby rocks the funk shaking her
    celestial booty I will now confess

I just go all kinds of crazy in my junk & as Bootsy struts
    his starry bass lines all through P-Funk

My old life as a CBGB punk seems so completely defunct
    & I'm just happy I'm still the one who's
    taking home the booty

Those nights my baby rocks the funk

THE ONE WHO SHOULD WRITE MY ELEGY IS DEAD

The one who should write my elegy is dead

When we made that bet he said most likely
    I'd be the loser writing his elegy instead

Nothing is as beautiful as nothing he once said
    so hip just chain-smoking Camels or

Riding his shaky Triumph up Van Ness & the one
    who should write my elegy is dead

I guess I always knew I'd have to write my own
    elegy for him instead

Rimbaud on a tractor Anna says or Jagger pirouetting
    through the ranch's drying shed

The one who should write my elegy is dead
    so I won't rehearse again those

Hungers that we fed or expose both the cruelties
    & those we shared

I'll simply try again to finish writing this last elegy
    instead of looking back & tonight

My daughter Vivienne's off with friends & Anna's
    reading of all things *Winter Stars* in bed

& the one who should write my elegy is dead & I'm
    the one the loser left here just as

He said I'd be left here writing his elegy instead

VINEYARD

You see a man walking the lanes & aisles
    of his vineyard & now

The spring tendrils stretch beyond his reach
    & you see too there's a black dog

Beside him a blissful Lab who slices across
    a horizon still white with dawn

You see this landscape is the landscape of
    my valley the one I remember

Out of the plunder that is the swollen glow
    of reflection & so to you I'll say

That a man is walking & I'll tell you now he's
    an older man & do you see his son

Behind him only nineteen or twenty no more his
    wool sweater wrapped

Around him the color of the dust at his feet
    a rich gold without equal

& now the sun begins to rub itself across
    the sky & this is the dog's life

Yet also the man's as well & he knows soon
    this boy will be leaving the valley

With a girl even younger than his son
    in a silver Pontiac LeMans

North along Highway 99 north all the way
        until they cross into Canada

Where anyone who wants to send his son
        to die won't be able to find him

& so there among the aisles & lanes & heavy
        grapes the father stops & the dog

Stops to turn & face the boy who drags a hand
        slowly along the Lab's silky head

& quietly wraps his skinny arms around his father
        & in the vineyard dust that's all

LUCKY

After a week of long winds & rain the sun broke from the Sierras
    & I sat on the porch watching

The dark tables of turned-under corn & tall alfalfa
    & the dead glistening grasses

Across the road the wide field & the abandoned house
    I'm walking to

Months vacant & paint-flaked now a place where kids
    come to drink & fuck

The weather-pocked shed down to its bones its skin ripped up
    for firewood

In the back garbage still scattered & waiting to be carted off
    or buried   the grass below it given up

I look in the glassless window & on the floor just a striped
    blood-brown mattress & empty green wine

& rust-colored beer bottles a few old rippled magazines
    & in the corner

The body of a hen her head broken to one side her back
    flat to the floor legs up the low

Underside of her belly eaten open—white feathers at wound's
    edge still curled over the dry rim

The whole guts of the crater stony gray & stiff the half-
    gnawed entrails black

*

Now this afternoon in the cold late-day sunlight

I have come to pick the roses at the front of the abandoned house
    grown wild in their winter bloom & tangled

Thick as nests as the thin branches of the climbers arc in long trails
    across the yard their pink babies' fists

Beating on the wind & along the broken picket fence the green
    all hung with rose-stars—scarlet or crimson

All the blushes of red—& a few struck white & one the color
    of peach flesh or apricot

& pairs of small yellow lips & others burnt golden & three like melons
    thick-petaled dim suns & in each bush the dark

Stiff-stemmed rose hips nodding like skulls

*

That night when my headlights hit the front of the old house

She came from its far side running through the wall
    of roses choking & biting on the air

As she made it finally to my car where I stood at the open
        driver's door brought by her screams

The rifle I'd pulled from above the mantel crooked in my elbow

The boys who'd been inside the house crashing out the back
        & peeling out in their midnight Cutlass

Back to Clovis or Selma

Sixteen & thrown out of everywhere for good & living sometimes
        with her grandparents in the foothills

She was down for a dance & then just a ride to get some beer
        it'd happened before she said & once with six

She says it closing her eyes

Then Lucky she says her name is Lucky combs out petals
        & crushed rose hips that float down

Sticking to her black angora sweater some torn petals
        she can't brush away   white hen petals

Dark rose feathers

GENERATION

Trust me I'm really trying to pay attention
    but it's harder every day

& so I begin to trust only in appearances not
    "authenticity"—that half truth—

Growing so precisely redacted it's even less
    now than what it once seemed

So I can't help it & maybe I'm doing all right?—
    someone else has to tell me

I spend all my time in meetings & almost none
    with the few people I love

Still my house is beautiful it's filled with books
    & filled with light & filled too

With eloquent recordings of music at the end
    of the world & also with the grace

Of the woman who's made this house of paper
    songs & tied my hand-inked messages

With black ribbons to those thin branches
    above the brick walkway

Leading to our door as it's now the single way
    I'll actually write to people

& how do I look to you these days?—& really
who remembers it all as you do?—

& when the night-blooming jasmine smells so
delicious I love just sitting here

Shredding on Lance's custom shop Les Paul—
my vintage Vox amp cranked up

So high no microphone could salvage those lyrics
of pure human spittle   you know

That song I mean the one about all of us—fiercely
irrelevant & yet so briefly alive

THE LAST TROUBADOUR

Standing at the glass-paneled wall of Liza's kitchen
    at the old house half-hidden

Over a mile up Canyon Road in Joshua's gated compound

I'm just smoking a joint & looking down at the dusk
    dusting the Malibu lights as they flare

Along the coastline below & I can hear the ripped-up

Buick fenders & Caddy bumpers slammed around out
    in the barn studio as they're slowly

Torched into art as Joshua moves the spitting arc-welder

Over armatures of rebar shaping a dozen abstract
    guitars or mandolins while its

Acetylene tongue ticks in the black shade of his visor

Once in a while his back-in-the-day transistor radio
    hooked on a nail bent in the wall

Cuts through the sizzle with a hit of his that's slipped

Lately back into fashion & I've watched him slowly lift
    the head of that torch until it angles

Against the turquoise plastic moon of the radio dial

As if he might melt it all back to a few black platters
    —those times as lost as song

ALEXANDR BLOK

One snowy night I was smiled upon by Russian gods
    & found myself at dinner opposite

The Moscow scholars a married couple—*he* only
    the world's authority on Pasternak

& *she* the final word on her beloved Alexandr Blok
    & as we talked the evening gathered

Along the length of the white table & I could only keep
    drinking the conversation in so deeply

I felt myself reaching back into the dark century & at last
    I got up to leave in my black cashmere

Overcoat I'd found hanging on the back rack of a Venice
    thrift store & became just another shadow

About to slide wordlessly into the night & yes it's true
    it was snowing just in upstate New York

Not Moscow or St. Petersburg nor in any ancient page
    yet to anyone who saw me walking

I imagined myself as the most lyrical shadow alive

TO A STORY

We'd become friends after I rented the empty studio
    behind her redwood house in Tiburon

As soon as she asked if I was good with my hands
    I understood she had a few things

That might need fixing around the place including
    her Jag convertible an old '54 XK120

Aged to a dull bullet-silver by the salty Bay air
    the walnut dash framing those twin

Disks of its black gauges   speedometer & tach
    & you know there's nothing I love

Like an elegant restoration in loving progress
    —stop giving me that look—

Her ex-husband Edison had even left a few berets
    in the closet hung above his oil paints

& I loved that old studio its raw uneven redwood
    planks letting in the soft fog at night

As well as those delicate early Brahms sonatas
    she'd practice as her ritual before

Leaving on tour & then always away a month or more
    so I'd watch the place & bring in the mail

& guard her koi pond from skinny dog-sized raccoons
    cruising up the narrow lanes at night

One morning she called out of the blue on her layover
     in Reykjavik & just started screaming

How *Esquire* had a story in it about her—not one of
     those devoted profiles she knew well

But a piece of actual fiction—*A story about her! by Edison*
     & she hated him truly

After letting him get away with endless affairs & years
     of good drugs & bad rehab she'd paid for

—& finally he'd gone too far   he'd made her into
     nothing but a story & worse claimed

She'd been older than she was when they first met
     & now she was screaming so loudly

I'm pretty sure most of Iceland could hear her say
     That fucking bastard even made me

Throw out the black panties Keith Richards signed for me
     & I said Ilaria!   just focus!—

Everybody knows Edison's a liar!   & then a long
     silence exquisitely cold as Reykjavik

Before I heard   *I am going now to catch my plane*
     more silence & then   *Don't leave me*

MY LIFE AS SANDOZ MESCALINE
(Bolinas Snapshot, 1972)

Jade lifted her face just briefly from the mirror she'd lined
    with a few pink hexagrams of

Sandoz mescaline & said vaguely to her devotees sprawled nude

On a lush Turkish rug *You know I'm sick of the "dystopian novel"*
    & we all nodded even the one guy

In the room who'd actually written one & Jade looked up in cool

Disdain adding   *I mean that fucking phrase: "dystopian novel"*
    not any of you sweethearts

& I was thrown into the depths of Darwinian despair as she looked

Straight at me saying *Lately only one thing gets me off* so I'm forever
    grateful to my friend Reggie for

Smoothing the rough skin of a drumhead to toss his Inuit divination

Dice—six miniature-carved-ivory huskies with rubbed violet coats
    all of them rolling & tumbling

& landing on the drumhead perfectly upright on all four paws

Subtly assembling into the very finest arctic dog team ever known
    anywhere close to Bolinas California

& in one somatic heartbeat I'd harnessed my spoon-sized sled

To their oracular dancing bodies & in an instant like night fog
    I was gone

EVANGELINE & HER SISTERS

I was a good hour beyond Oxford
     & nearly to Clarksdale

& looking for that roadhouse where
     Evangeline promised she'd be

Waiting she said until I showed up with
     her 1937 National Tricone

& got at least a little of the money she'd
     owed me since Ohio maybe even

Morgantown I can't remember anymore
     except that I do know the reasons

She'd pull out those skinny twin silver
     .38s she had a habit of always

Introducing as *My Sisters* & then level them
     at the boyish clerks counting

Out the stiff bills she'd so politely requested
     & there was nobody ever who

Didn't know she was a distinguished personage
     & to always call her ma'am

AN ECCLESIASTICAL SKETCHBOOK

Let learning be simple chalk and slate, corrugate
flags of a late republic
terror of form,
in the line of a breast to bony hip:
again ecclesiastic . . .

—NORMAN DUBIE

Here is the way no longer lost yet still so often
     unremarked upon & which recalls

Those old lessons of a hand as it insinuates its stroke
     along the sketchbook's rough page   & if

Reverie is a state beyond all forms allowed by the state

This sweetness of dawn psalm claws at the lovers' lips
     even in the sweat of nakedness—

These days becoming so much less than we once believed—

& as Raphael draws the tip of his brush along the breasts
     of the baker's daughter for whom he'd forsaken

A cardinal's scarlet robes & though he died with Margarita's
     portrait unfinished only days after

Inhaling the poisoned air of a newly opened Roman tomb
　　we try to learn again every way

Art remains a last sanctified artifice of home although

We can't help but taste how even our desires falter
　　as the body falls to its altar

ABOVE SUNSET

All the hippest ghouls are out tonight along the boulevard
      the day calls Sunset

& she's the loveliest dead girl in sight her skin powdered blank
      as China White with a torn red bustier

& kohl leather jacket & all the hippest ghouls are just
      digging it tonight

Amazed she's stepped out at last beneath these bright piercing
      klieg lights . . . & in all this neon racket

She's still the loveliest dead girl in sight walking right beside me
      holding on tight to balance spiked heels

& spiked hair—*black-jet*—& all the ghouls parading
      Sunset tonight turn as she passes

A few even weeping in delight though the tourists look appalled . . .
      fuck it—she's mine & the loveliest dead girl

In sight & now on her bedroom balcony as sails of dawn light
      sift along the whitening hills above Sunset

We're the happiest ghouls of the night & she's still the dead-
      loveliest dead girl in sight

BACKSTREETS

It was a backstreet cutting off from Rue Saint-Jacques & most
    of the apartments were shuttered still

Against the brisk blades of early morning the sills of a few
    lined with green wood window boxes

Of anemones or dahlias here or there blue geraniums & lilies
    & on Roxanne's second-floor balcony

Just outside its open brass doors the tarnished antique cage
    still swaying slightly on its hook

As her mustard-colored finch worked its way up a sequence
    of perches brushing each wing

Along the cage's wires each as fragile as the bird's own bones
    & as I turned a corner losing sight of Roxy's

For no reason I could imagine except my long-awaited absence
    her goldfinch began to sing

EQUIVALENTS

It was a sentimental time in my life & I carried
  my Leica with me everywhere

Its silver fittings blacked-out with electrical tape
  just the way I'd seen Cartier-Bresson's

& I only listened to the best so when Frederick told me
  don't read Freud & I asked Why not?

He'd said *You'll end up just like me every time I say*
  "soul" I really mean "libido"

I wasn't worried & I'd pinned on my wall a wrinkled
  proof he'd tossed out—a nude of X—its

Surface scarred by wood tongs as he'd yanked it up
  out of its bath a little drunk

I loved that shot & the near erasure of skin lightly over-
  exposed so her body

Rippled into currents of light as she held up an empty
  & bent rectangle of brass

She'd saved from the trash pile in their studio lifting
  it level with her breasts

To frame a whole century of assumptions she'd already
  begun dissolving in her

Own radical revisions of the light—a porous sculpted skull
    & horse collar of pelvic bones

Bleached whiter & more luminous than any negative cold zero
    of the desert night

APERTURE

She was a doorway
Opening onto the light

She was the light
Within this doorway

She stood like the single
Aperture of the night

A last molded pupil
Of flesh

Dilated entirely by
The absolute & eloquent

Profile of
Desire

      ★

A doorway at
The tunnel of the body

More luminous
Than the mind

Where he stood before her
Every filament ablaze

Every lens of
Consciousness et cetera

★

The molten speed of a moment
Signaling the arrival

Bodies upon a shifting
Plain of stars

So blank not even the shadow
Of the moon might arrive

Without the suture
Of surprise

EMANATIONS

—Jeffers Country

As the trees conspired toward evening I walked below the tor
     its long grass edged & interrupted by rock

& low bracken in an air sifted by the sea's scent powdered
     by kelp & foam   Jeffers said

Of Weston as he might have said exactly of himself it takes great
     strength to believe truly

In solitude trusting its sinews & silence holding yourself against
     waves of your own darkness

     ★

I was taking Evangeline to rehab in Pacific Grove twenty years ago
     a place near Point Pinos Lighthouse

Lance had just moved to a new manse in Carmel at Scenic & Stewart
     & he'd said to come by because

He was right by Tor House & he was pretty sure I could find my way

& when I arrived I saw Jimi the Lion there & Cissie too & I yelled into
     the kitchen where Lance was swirling

Pasta in a pan & finally as I made my way to greet him I saw just
     past the kitchen patio not

Thirty feet beyond his window those huge looming eggs of stone
    the granite boulders Jeffers

Hauled & rolled from the shore beyond the tor every afternoon
    its medieval & majestic power

One whole side of Hawk Tower stolidly ascending in front of me
    & sometimes

The land can seem as harsh or even harsher than a skeptical man
    who walks mornings not speaking

The world's raw sea edge awaiting him—he who slowly made
    stone love stone

           ★

There's a photo of my namesake son at eight beside me as we follow
    the trail to Pinnacle Rock

& Cypress Grove on his first visit to Point Lobos exactly the age I was
    when first there with my aunt

& I remember feeling like the father I wasn't until that day my son
    & I stood together above those lethal rocks

Smashed by purposeful waves & those skyrocket cathedrals of spray

           ★

Above Castro Creek a redwood circle illumined—its lichen lit
     by sunlight

An early silence & the day is released along the whole length
     of Castro Canyon   Anna's waking

Beneath the skylight of our cabin as outside the birds unchain
     again the many swaying promises of limbs

Within those nearby pines & naturally in this room beyond

    *

Last night feeling as random as the rain . . . I read in *Daybooks*
     Weston praising Jeffers & that fierce pulse

Weston called the resurgent will of the natural world & I thought
     of Anna yesterday

Approached by a doe & curious fawns walking the circumference
     of Whalers Cove

& last week returning along the high cliffside trail from China Cove
     we'd stopped so I could shoot all

Point Lobos fanned out & ragged—its exquisite prospects rising up
     & just below us a discrete pebble beach

& familiar tide pools where Ansel Adams told anyone who'd listen
     must one day be named Weston Beach

& so it was   & so it is

*

The summer I turned sixteen visiting my aunt in the skylit studio
    she'd built onto the cottage

In my grandmother's landscaped garden among rose beds & curved
    lawns & tall candles of iris—& as

We talked across the rising perfume of turpentine & fresh oils my aunt
    turned from the canvas

She'd been painting of the Santa Lucia Range & paused a moment
    handing me

A birthday gift a fresh hardcover of *Not Man Apart* with Jeffers's poems
    & images of Big Sur's coast

& she opened the book to a photograph by Weston of the familiar cove
    its surly rocks & twisted kelp & pebbles

& asked *Do you remember the day I took you here? That man who called
    out hello with the tripod & box camera was*

Weston's son—my gorgeous old Graflex I always use & love was his once

*

A few years after Lance moved from his place down along
      Yankee Point up to the Highlands

We rendezvoused in Carmel & I followed him past the turnoff
      leading to Weston's house on Wildcat Hill

Until we looped up Mal Paso onto San Remo & then we all just
      sat watching

That scarlet sunset fan dance over the Pacific's darkening jade

      ★

For years I'd kept a notebook of obscure trails between Point Lobos
      & Gorda all those glories

Of both Big & Little Sur but that morning we decided let's be obvious
      & drove down toward McWay Falls

Stopping on the roadside to spend time along Partington Cove Trail

—I broke stride a moment as above the meadow in the dense pines
      a shadow cross

Hung overhead barely clearing the pines' tips a silent condor just
      arcing away

The span of its wings ten feet one fan-feathered tip to the other

      ★

I grew up in a house of redwood glass & stone the house my mother
  built from Cliff May's blueprints

A lesson in organic mid-century modern aspiration huge exposed
  beams of solid redwood its ceiling planks too

The fireplace a mosaic of flagstones & multicolored volcanic rocks
  & living room walls pale Australian gum

A house that could comfortably have fit in Mill Valley or Carmel
  yet somehow also in the arid San Joaquin

The Fresno of my childhood where it stood as testament to possibility
  —my California of the '50s

    ★

Today we walked down to Henry Miller's library to steal Wi-Fi
  & sit with an espresso

—as news of the world came a hawk overhead dipped one wing

So I turned off my phone & opened *The Air-Conditioned Nightmare*
  & that's all the irony anyone should share

    ★

In 1936 a hundred miles south of these rock crags sloping low & falling
  abruptly off into the Pacific

Charis drove Weston to Oceano & its miles of dunes so he could plant
    his 8 x 10 Century Universal camera on its skinny tripod

Into the sands & one day Charis sunbathing nude decided simply to roll
    down the face of one dune & another

& so posing for Edward the Spy those hours & days while they stayed
    in Gavin Arthur's (see *The Circle of Sex*)

Old beach shack & this morning I awoke thinking of Charis driving back
    up Highway 1 along the coast

Past Morro Rock & Moonstone Beach past Piedras Blancas & Lucia
    & up over Bixby Creek then to the Highlands

All the way to Wildcat Hill & the swarm of felines tame & feral & then
    Edward making coffee

As she began slicing the apples she'd left on the wood counter to ripen
    & now emanations

Of naked Edenic fruits were scenting the whole length of the room

Its bare redwood planks & ripening apple flesh held in late dusk
    & the wood stove

Heated up as Charis knelt to feed more limbs to its belly & she knew
    these next days in the darkroom

They would bring to paper this sequence of nudes her body white on
    white against Oceano's dunes

Her final acquiescence & reverence for skin married to a future light

     *

One day last fall I went to Tor House early to be alone a few hours
    before the tours began

& climb the stairs of Hawk Tower in solitude & later stand in silence
    by the bed *by the sea-window*

Jeffers chose as *a good death-bed* thirty years before the fact to see

The pulse of waves licking raw the shore stones as pines & cypress
    chimed in the sea wind

     *

It hardly matters to anyone but me how sometimes as I walk this coast
    Point Pinos Point Lobos Point Sur   I'm singing

South Coast the wild coast is lonely . . . the lion still rules the barranca
    & a man there is always alone

THE DARKROOM

In negative both body & sand graduate only slightly any pure black
they've recovered from the light

Revealing as the prints emerge in their basin once again the way
a simple swirl of flesh

Across the grained vanilla of the beach allows for sensual waves
rising & falling breaking

Free of my own misunderstanding of the day & your own as well
& because light's a most complex companion

& the most fluent & most amused by touching only what it wishes
to expose

Obscuring anything it's chosen to refuse or grown bored by just
slipping off into its own shadow left opaque

& pale as those expectant ghosts in the dregs of my espresso cup
tossed out nonchalantly into the wet street

By a waiter watching us walk away from this café into an evening
of sudden dark curtains & a platinum spring rain

THE STONES OF VENICE

She was the first person ever in my life to tell me
     of the many complicated ways

John Ruskin had for years given her sleepless nights

& I admit I really didn't have a good comeback line
     —I began to feel a little like Robert Dudley

Kneeling before Elizabeth on a path at Kew Gardens

Looking for the pearl button he'd accidentally bitten
     off a sleeve of her sculpted velvet dress

& I know most things need not devolve to the devotional

So finally I just flew home from London to Baltimore
     & soon after she called to say she'd

Put to bed at last the final pages of her Ruskin book
     & was delighted to report to me

She'd absolutely nailed it with *The Stones of Venice* chapter
     about which she'd been brilliant she confessed

& I smiled only a moment with a pearl bit between my teeth

SILVER & BLACK

In those days Jesse still worked in the movies as
        the assistant to a cool producer

Who'd courted Jet Li before he was anybody here
        & to show his stuff Jet Li'd kicked

A hanging begonia out of its macramé & wire basket
        on the porch of their office at Universal

She told me laughing over the red sauce she'd made
        the way her mama would she swore pouring

A little extra red wine into the pan then a little more
        & she was so shy she blushed every time

I teased her friends the gorgeous boys who hung out
        with her crew of rock-steady girls all

Drop-dead slinky beauties still looking for a break
        & I wished them well each one of them

& after they'd leave we'd sit back on her leather sofa
        black like every piece of her furniture & walls

With a few alarming slashes of silver accent now & then
        & it felt exactly like living in an old Thirties

Noir classic where every one of our nights was steamy
        but always lost in a black-&-silver sorrow

There were even a few blank silver birthday balloons
   floating against the ceiling above the bed

& at times like that it could seem all of Sicily unfolded
   across her face & pooled beneath her

Eyes dark as the distance she'd come from Selinunte
   & the dirt of her family fields & those

Early graves & wrapped in those black sheets with silver
   pillows piled around us I kept trying

To find some great consoling exit line of dialogue she
   hadn't already read not even in those scripts

Scattered on the floor of her bedroom not even the one
   she said was really about me holding it up

With one hand—a hipster slacker indie remake of
   the 1933 horror classic by H. G. Wells

With Claude Rains playing my favorite part of course
   one I knew by heart   *The Invisible Man*

PASTERNAK & THE SNOWY HERON

It should have been easy to pull the plow from the marsh
  now the thaw has settled in but

It took two men & the plow horse all working together
  to finally clear it at last

That was what Stella read aloud to me as she flipped through
  those letters her mother had sent

After her father died & her brothers left Moscow for Canada
  & she left finally too

& I should have known when she boarded the Montrealer in her
  Zhivago coat—all the rage that year

Yet never right for a winter in Baltimore—& she'd left behind

The photograph framed & nailed by our bed of Pasternak alone
  at his desk in Peredelkino

A room spare as a monk's filled with snow-lit light & on one wall
  you could make out the print of

Audubon's great snowy heron standing in marsh grass its beak
  poised at an angle of fierce attention

Its eyes locked in that acute otherworldly focus of Pasternak's own—
  & she left too on the maple table

The tiny framed snapshot I'd taken: Stella holding up her truly
  beloved companion   *My Sister, Life*

My only copy I'd given to her the very one she'd spirited away

IN BANGKOK

My son wrote to me from Bangkok saying that when he'd arrived
    to have his ink done by

The legendary tattoo guru Jimmy Wong it wasn't the sounds of a city
    & its chaos that he'd minded

Though friends he'd made following the Ring of Fire complained of it
    —he wrote to me on one of those

Old-fashioned light-as-air blue folding envelopes in a darker blue
    script & said

Instead it was the steady silence of God in Bangkok that rang
    in his ears as the needle buzzed

In the hand of the revered artist duplicating the exact design my son
    himself had drawn to be inked

Across his thick right bicep the image of a world suddenly stilled
    a globe gripped in the talons

Of an ancient dragon that had seized its prey with a leer of silver fangs
    & the echo of a thousand

Years of silence upon silence upon God's silence rippling & deafening

The silence hollowing his own body as the needle etched the flesh
    & a rivulet of color seeped from his muscles

& he walked out of Jimmy's into Bangkok's clamor shaking still
    —the clapper of a just-rung temple bell

LITTLE SUR

As in the beginning the early tide at last collapses
      & recedes as porous knuckles of rock

Shoulder their way above the foam where cormorants
      drift & settle & as the day begins inhaling

These last wisps of morning fog & rags of sunlight
      lift into the redwoods rising up along

The canyon walls & in the inlet below us elephant seals
      announce their daily dawn arguments

With those lessons of pre-history & your hair floats across
      the bed as easily as strands of the ruby kelp

That just yesterday rose silently beside the kayak as you
      carved a singular quiet along the waking bay

TO THOSE WHO HAVE ASKED ANNA

To those who've asked Anna how it feels
    to know she'll likely die

Alone without her husband—meaning me—
    at her side for comfort as she

Nears some future ending which may or not
    bring with it some late solace

Though of course we never—any of us—know
    what awaits each of us alone

No matter who might stand by us briefly though
    I know as you might here in my faux

Venetian village by the Pacific where for two
    weeks more exactly I'm twice

Anna's age & yet young as I am to those who've
    asked Anna I have nothing to say

Not lit by a luminous certainty I'll be at peace
    only when those who've asked Anna

Are left at last alone & ripped by a silence bloody
    as August sky

DAMIAN'S TALE

Because I'd gotten there so early I'd grabbed a table right
    outside the Novel Café next

To a hip young couple meditating on decorative foam leaves
    floating atop their mega-lattes

& a quick glance pegged her as a devotee of another new hybrid
    Eco-Goth look one just had to love

Though he was a more standard-issue Santa Monica surf stud
    in pale blond cords & curls

& the same smoky blue plaid Pendleton the Beach Boys wore
    then Damian pulled up

Straight from the airport in what seemed the smallest rentable
    sub-sub-compact I'd ever seen

& slowly unfolded his six-foot-six collapsible L.A. Laker's body
    & stood up rail-straight looking

At me grinning while I just shook my head & pretty soon we were
    contemplating our own foamy leaves

& talking about some lines of Sophocles he'd been translating
    that morning as the deadline

For his book got near & as we both put our intellects on pause
    sipping our lattes in that momentary silence

We heard the girl say consolingly *of course I always think about*
    you when I'm masturbating well

Almost always not always maybe but really most of the time—
    so after that I admit

It was hard to go back to talking about versions of Sophocles
    but Damian soldiered on

Telling me a girl he'd loved in his twenties had just written to say
    she still thought of him a lot

Yet it wasn't anything he imagined she'd remember—it was the way
    he'd rested his hands on the yellow keys

Of a broken-down Yamaha upright in his old Chestnut St. apartment
    & after finishing a piece

Would reach over & touch the earlobe of her right ear with one finger
    & so he said we just never know

What makes lovers into lovers after all & what surprised him most
    was that after all these years she'd taken

The time simply taken her time that she'd taken time at last to write

THE OLD WAVE

I listened as my old friend began reciting aloud the Sutra
    of the Old Wave—

She'd lived a monk's life at Tassajara & then Rome & Santa Fe
    & the joy she stitched around her

In the sounds of the Old Wave reminded me the way an elegant
    silence would cocoon her body

Easily as rain collects invisibly into a necklace of pools along a path
    after a spring storm

One night in Rome I photographed her standing in Piazza Santa Maria
    still & poised as the nearby Virgin

& only weeks later I gave her the print asking what she was thinking
    that moment & she

Looked entirely amused & I wasn't at all surprised she'd answered—
    why   just nothing

Her laughter was origami unfolding or the steady pulse of Solovyov's
    mystic white lily

As her body was gathered up into the Sutra of the Old Wave

THE BLACK JAGUAR

Finally today I took a long walk down to Houston so
    I could see friends

After a week trapped in the sorry canyons of Midtown so

I walked around Nolita just trying to find the place Veronique
    & I first lived

After she'd joined me from Trastevere & one day over coffee
    I'd explained myself to her—

This was *this way* & That was *that* & she looked at me saying
    oh poor boy   lost in

Opposites held so close around you like some thin winter coat

& it made sense at the time even though she herself wore only
    her trademark

Black astrakhan bolero to keep warm during those hard nights
    & I miss those days in Rome

Living almost as in an Antonioni movie & then a tiny black cat

Svelte as a toy jaguar on my old fire escape starts howling down
    to some alley toms

Howling back up at her & if Veronique were here she'd say *oh*
    tu cose povere   calma tutti   everything's ok—

SCRIPT FOR THE LOST REFLECTION

Walking the shore road making my way along the water
    I keep thinking of the ways

An aperture opens to the light even as day darkens—

These days I carry only what I can touch & touch only
    what brings me focus

I mean interior focus an old shadow-&-wick sense & I've

Brought those photographs you'd asked for so you'll explain
    just what you meant

One night you told me *a way to see is a way to live*

Everything in me looks to believe you as I hold myself against
    the body

Equivalent to the world's body even as your breath exhales

Across the sky like a negative held up against the gathering music
    of clouds

Scored to bring *the figure of the figure* back to the natural world

Until dust & lacunae arise as you lift your Rollei to sweep the cirrus
    the way Debussy

Set in motion the cursive whispers of the sky a graphic white on white

Over a script of black tapestries hung across this hypnotic translucence
    —strips of old negatives strewn

Across the sloping studio floor their ghostly shapes held in a sequence

Of frames no longer lit by fire & I'm exactly who I say I am tonight just
    an image

Of a last reflection fading slowly as summer light before your eyes

Notes

Emanations: With its tragic narrative, the song "South Coast" is the most well known song of early California, the era of *ranchos* and *vaqueros*, and the Monterey–Big Sur central coast area. A poem that was originally titled "The Coast Ballad," written in 1926 by Lillian Bos Ross, it became the basis of Ross's novel *The Stranger* (1942). That same year, Sam Eskin provided the melody to the original ballad and Richard Dehr and Frank Miller gave it an arrangement we now associate with "South Coast." The Kingston Trio did perhaps the most widely known recording of the song, although Ramblin' Jack Elliott's version is without peer.

I've chosen not to include work from two stand-alone volumes, the book-length sonnet sequence *Prism* and the book *The Face: A Novella in Verse*. Also, poems from two collections of previously "uncollected" poems, *In the Pines: Lost Poems, 1972–1997* and *The Window: Poems, 1998–2012,* have been omitted from this collection.

In memoriam—These poems are also dedicated to the memory of: Italo Calvino; Galway Kinnell; Philip Levine; Larry Levis; Adrienne Rich; Mark Strand; and C. K. Williams.